Probably Magic
The Wedding Quilt

Book Five of The Probably Magic Series

Jo Jewell

The Wedding Quilt by Jo Jowell
Copyright © 2021. All rights reserved.

ALL RIGHTS RESERVED: No part of this book may be reproduced, stored, or transmitted, in any form, without the express and prior permission in writing of Pen It! Publications, LLC. This book may not be circulated in any form of binding or cover other than that in which it is currently published.

This book is licensed for your personal enjoyment only. All rights are reserved. Pen It! Publications does not grant you rights to resell or distribute this book without prior written consent of both Pen It! Publications and the copyright owner of this book. This book must not be copied, transferred, sold or distributed in any way.

Disclaimer: Neither Pen It! Publications, or our authors will be responsible for repercussions to anyone who utilizes the subject of this book for illegal, immoral or unethical use.

This is a work of fiction. The views expressed herein do not necessarily reflect that of the publisher.

This book or part thereof may not be reproduced in any form, stored in a retrieval system, or transmitted in any form by any means-electronic, mechanical, photocopy, recording or otherwise- without prior written consent of the publisher, except as provided by United States of America copyright law.

Published by Pen It! Publications, LLC in the U.S.A.
812-371-4128
www.penitpublications.com

ISBN: 978-1-63984-037-3
Edited by Wanda Williams
Cover Design by Donna Cook

Dedication

To all Holocaust Victims and Survivors
and
Those who strive to keep history from repeating this atrocity.

Acknowledgments

I have to tell you; I had no idea it would be so hard to write this book. As I learned more and more about the Holocaust, I found myself on a roller coaster of tears, anger, helplessness, and fear. Fear that as our society strives to erase and rewrite history to be less uncomfortable, we will become immune to such tragic entries to history and history being, by its own nature, a repeat of the past.

Probably Magic learns an important lesson about compassion. It changes everything.

I hope, when you read this book, you will notice how a small change in how we view events in our lives, can have a profound effect on how we conduct ourselves.

I would like to thank Pen It! Publications for being my publisher, Wanda Williams for her endless patience with me, Ruth Lewallen for her unwavering support, and Carmine Hudson for being willing to keep me straight as I ramble on and on telling a story. I also want to thank my sister, Carol Davis for constantly asking, "What's happening now? Do Wally and Probably get married?" I refused to give her any spoiler alerts and she called me a brat. Yep, I'm a brat.

I also thank God for allowing me to write this book. On November 5th, 2020, I was told I am going blind. I was so afraid I would not be able to finish writing The Wedding Quilt. I did finish it and have started making the adjustments I will need to make if I am to continue sharing stories with you.

God Bless you all richly and thank you for joining me on this adventure. You are loved and appreciated.

April 15, 1943
Klamry, Poland

Vesta tied off the last knot and broke the thread with her teeth. Her glasses did not help her eyesight but they were better than nothing. She raised her head and listened. She did that often these days. One never knew when the gunshots would be right outside your door. One never knew when the knock on the door meant **Maveth** (Death) had arrived.

She heard footsteps. She didn't fear these footsteps though. They were heavy steps with a bit of an off-rhythm from a slight limp. They belonged to her beloved husband Jacob. She listened for the inner foyer door to open.

"Mama! I'm home!" he called out to her. They announced themselves so they would know it wasn't a German Soldier.

She lay her sewing aside and stood to greet him. He gave her a peck on the cheek and asked what was for supper.

"I was so lucky today!" she said with great excitement, "Toadee had extra turnips and four potatoes. I used a bone broth and made us a fine stew today."

Jacob boyishly smacked his lips and smiled, "I can hardly wait. Let me go wash up first, Mama."

As they sat eating their meager meal, Vesta told him she had finally finished the Wedding Quilt. "I don't know when I'll be able to ship it to Leah though. With this war, everything is out of kilter. It feels like she's halfway around the world!"

Jacob laughed, "She IS halfway around the world, Mama! Leah will appreciate it when she gets it. Have you heard from her lately?"

"Oh, she is very busy. Her husband is in banking and works long hours. Poor Leah must tend to baby Maria while Elizabeth works in a factory. She says Michigan is helping with the war effort but I don't know what that means. How I wish I could be with her to help."

Jacob patted her hand. He was troubled but he would not show it to his wife. He had protected her for forty-nine years. They would soon be celebrating their fiftieth. He prayed daily they would be alive for that glorious celebration.

"How was work today?" she asked as she finished sopping the stew with bread.

"My bones say it was a long day," he smiled. "My soul says it was a tiring day. I'm not as young as I used to be."

"Oh, Jacob, you've worked so hard all our lives. I wish you could not work and we would be okay," she sighed.

"Don't you worry, Mama, I will always provide and care for you," he assured her. "Let's say our evening prayers and go to bed. I just want to hold you close."

She blushed and hurried to straighten the kitchen. When she sat down in the living room, Jacob lit a candle and bowed his head in servitude. He looked up as she settled in her chair.

He smiled and they said in unison, holding hands, heads bowed.

In the name of Adonai the God of Israel
May the Angle Michael be at my right,
And the Angel Gabriel be at my left,
And in front of me the Angel Uriel.

And behind me the Angel Raphael…
And above my head the Sh'khinah.

With reverence, they blew out the candle together and walked to the bedroom. When they were settled in the bed, Jacob put his arms around his wife and held her close. He could not help it, the tears slipped from his eyes. He feared their time was short. He heard horrible rumors among the workers at the slaughterhouse. Rumors that Hitler was making his way across Poland leaving death and destruction in his path. Rumors that trains gathered Polish and French Jews who were never to be seen again. He hoped all that was not true but, in his heart, he knew better. He felt Vesta take a deep breath.

In the morning, Vesta rose before Jacob. She fixed a breakfast of oatmeal and the last slice of bread. For his lunch, she gave him the leftover bone broth stew. She bit her lower lip trying to think of what else she could add to his lunch. She rummaged in the icebox and found a pear. It was bruised on one side and a bit on the soft side but it could be very good with the stew. She put a chunk of cheese wrapped in cheesecloth in the metal lunchbox and stood back satisfied.

Jacob came into the kitchen and wished her good morning. She reached up and touched the yellow Star of David on his jacket. He took her hand in his and kissed it.

"If you go out, be very careful," he warned. "This war has made our day-to-day lives very unpredictable. Always be aware."

"I will Papa. You be careful too!" she said.

Such were their lives. While they praised God and gave thanks for each day they were gifted, still, the worry and constant vigilance stole the color from the days, brightness from the smiles, and openness from their faces. Life had become a palette of grays, browns, slate blue, and suspicion.

She said a prayer of protection as her husband left for work. She returned to the wedding quilt and looked at it with longing. A stout tradition, steeped in ritual and thanksgiving, the quilt had taken a long time to reach her from her mother, now bent with age and fingers gnarled from a lifetime of hard work. The pink roses were the promise of a loving marriage, the intertwining vines for the hope of many healthy children, the Star of David meant martyrdom, the wavy lines brought strength when matrimonial waters became choppy. Then, perhaps, the most striking feature of all, the name of each new wife that was gifted the quilt. Sure, through the years, certain things had to be repaired or replaced but the love of each stitch, each testament, was there.

Vesta added a special touch of her own. She had written a letter to Leah. She hoped it conveyed hope in these uncertain times and peace should she not see tomorrow's sunrise.

She carefully wrapped the quilt and hid it in a secret cupboard in the tiny dining room. She hoped it would be safe and if anything should happen to her and Jacob, that it would find its way to Leah. One just never knew. One just kept faith in God and trusted He knew best.

Another day passed while she busied herself scurrying to the market to see what food she could afford for the evening meal. She found a piece of chocolate that was marked into four squares! She shouldn't spend what little money they had on such frivolous non-essentials but she just couldn't resist. She bought a small chicken, two potatoes, and compensated by not buying bread. She smiled all the way home.

"Sister Vesta!" she heard her name. Esther Polski waved at her to come closer.

"Vesta, I made bread today!" she announced. "For some reason, it made too many loaves. I would like to gift you two loaves of bread."

Vesta raised her eyes and thanked God for provisions but she felt bad taking two loaves, a very generous gesture to be sure when so many were trying to eke out enough for families with children. She must pay for the loaves. That was the only way she could accept them in good conscience. Her thoughts grudgingly went to the four squares of chocolate she so looked forward to surprising Jacob with but at the same time, bread was scarce and this was fresh!

"I will trade you two squares of chocolate for the two loaves," she said before she lost her nerve.

"Chocolate? Where did you come by chocolate? That would be a wonderful treat for the children!" Esther glowed with anticipation.

Vesta handed her two squares of chocolate and took the two loaves of bread. She thanked Esther profusely but her heart begrudged the two squares of chocolate. At least she and Jacob could have one square each but she knew in her heart of hearts that she would only take the smallest taste and give the rest to her beloved.

That evening felt festive. They enjoyed the chicken, boiled potatoes, and fresh bread with butter fresh from the churn. Jacob told funny stories from his work and they laughed together. After the meal, Vesta presented Jacob with the chocolate. His eyes became wide as he stared in disbelief.

"Vesta! We cannot afford such luxuries!" he chastised her.

"No! I had four squares but Esther offered me two loaves of fresh bread for two squares of chocolate. So, see? I got everything we needed for our evening meal and still was able to treat us. You work so hard, Jacob. You deserve a treat now and then," she spoke but she could feel the tears in her eyes.

"You are a good woman, Vesta. I'm sorry I reacted so badly. It's just times are so…"

"I know. It will make it even sweeter on the tongue," she said softly and handed him the full two squares of chocolate.

He handed her one square and they took the smallest of nibbles from the delicacy and then wrapped them to save for later. They would make it last as long as possible.

They said their evening prayers and Vesta silently asked for forgiveness for begrudging Esther the chocolate in payment for the bread. They went to bed and Jacob extinguished the lamp next to the bed and then turned to his wife. It was almost like when they were first married. She slept in contentment while the war raged outside their door but she was at peace with the man who loved her.

The next morning, they went through their morning ritual. She hid a tiny piece of chocolate in Jacob's lunch pail and giggled when she thought of him finding it tucked away. Jacob kissed her and once again urged her to be safe and smiling, he turned to her and said, "And no extra surprises today, my love. You'll have me expecting such extravagances all the time!" She laughed with him.

As he reached the front door, it suddenly flew open knocking him backward from the impact. Vesta didn't even have time to react. The German soldiers swarmed into the tiny apartment and grabbed Vesta by the arm.

"We'll go with you!" Jacob shouted, "Please! Don't hurt her!"

Vesta's face was distorted with terror. Jacob began to silently cry as the soldiers roughly pushed them down the stairs and out onto the street. On either side of the street Jews were lined up single file. Vesta saw the young family from downstairs. They had an infant daughter and a five-year-old son. She saw Old Mr. Braun who always moved slowly, bent with twisted bones and aching feet. She saw her neighbor, Lina. Esther stood shivering with her two children trying to hide behind her skirts. They were all wide-eyed with fear, trembling under the unblinking eyes of the soldiers.

Jacob reached for Vesta's hand. He could feel her quaking. He squeezed it tighter.

"I love you, Vesta Krause. You have been the love of my life and all any man could ask for in a wife," he said softly. "Remember the chocolate. No matter what happens next, think of the joy of the chocolate."

She looked at him and nodded and closed her eyes.

They heard the click behind their heads.
"Schießen!" *(Shoot)*

Chapter One
2017

"For crying out loud, Red, read the next spin!" Wally yelled. I couldn't reach the spin board. Wally was wound up like a pretzel and Miss Vera was trying to maintain a certain amount of dignity and modesty by holding her skirt between her knees. That made it particularly rough since Right Hand Red and Yellow Left Foot were splayed across the play mat. If you ever see the game Twister at a yard sale, run. Run fast and don't look back.

I finally hooked the board with my right big toe and tried to inch it closer to me. Almost there. Just a breath away. I can do this! No, I can't. We fell in a laughing tangle of arms and legs. Miss Vera's glasses came off and we laughed even harder because no one could untangle enough to pick them up for her.

Once we caught our breath we sat on the floor with our backs against the furniture. Miss Vera was panting and fanning her face. Wally put his arm around me and kissed the top of my head.

"Good Lord! You young folks have more energy than me!" she exclaimed. "Who's ready for some ice-cold lemonade?"

Wally and I said, "I am!" in unison.

Miss Vera struggled to her feet by getting on her hands and knees and pulling herself up on the armchair.

"I love you," Wally whispered when Miss Vera disappeared.

I smiled, "I love you too. We say that a lot, don't we?"

Wally squeezed me close, "Yeah, we do. And I hope you don't get tired of hearing it because you're gonna hear it for the rest of your life."

Wally proposed to me on Christmas Day 2016. Miss Vera and I were enjoying a Christmas morning together when there was a knock on the door. I thought it would be Aunt Jo. I had no reason to think in a million years it would be anyone other than Aunt Jo. When I opened the door, there was Wally on one knee, holding a ring box, and asking me to marry him. I shut the door in his face.

Of course, people wanted to know if we had set a date and we just demurely declined to answer. The truth was, I was a little uncomfortable talking about a wedding, my wedding in particular. I know I should have been excited and giddy and running right out to buy every Bride's Magazine I could get my hands on but I couldn't. The cold, hard, unvarnished truth was, I was terrified. It was like I had absolutely no comprehension of the ceremony between lover and wife.

Miss Vera came in with a tray of tall glasses of frosty lemonade and homemade lemon bar cookies. Wally and I stood, taking a glass of the sweet lemony beverage and a lemon bar. Miss Vera was still laughing about our attempt at Twister.

"So, do we try it again or do I put it in the next yard sale?" I asked mischievously.

"Yard Sale!" they both laughed.

When spring came around, Wally helped me plant flowers and surprised me with a new garden bench. He talked about how on a hunch and raw curiosity he stopped at a yard sale. We started going every Saturday morning. It was fun! We bought things we definitely did not need, and some things we thought we needed, and every once in a while, we found exactly what we were looking for. And sometimes we bought stupid stuff…like Twister.

On this spring morning, I was getting the garden equipment ready so Corrie and I could plant a small vegetable garden. Corrie was now twelve years old and when most girls her age were secretly coveting cute boys and lip gloss, Corrie just wanted to be with Wally and me. I met Corrie and her mother on the very first indoctrination of my strange life. My very first spirit encounter was a Confederate soldier who came to me wanting me to deliver a love letter to the love of his life, Rosa Hargate. Of course, both had long since passed on but a descendant of Rosa was alive and well. Her name was also Rosa and she had a young daughter named Corinthia, Corrie in the shortened version. Her name for me was Skunk. We've been close ever since.

"Hey, Skunk! Guess what?" I heard her call out.

I looked up in time to see her race around the side of the house. A plastic bag bounced as she ran to me. Her face was beautiful in the morning sunshine.

She held up the bag, "I got rutabagas!"

"Do you even know what rutabagas are?" I asked her.

"No but it's fun to say!" she laughed. "We have carrots, peas, tomatoes, and rutabagas! Would you care for a Rutabaga sandwich?"

I couldn't help but laugh. Wally came down the back steps with his cup of tea. "Mornin', Trouble!"

Corrie ran to him and hugged him. "Guess what? We're gonna plant rutabagas!"

All at once, she stopped. The smile slipped from her face and she cocked her head.

"What's the matter?" I asked alarmed.

She stood still for a moment and looked around her.

"Corrie?" I tried to get her attention.

"That was weird," she said softly.

"What?"

"Did you feel it?" she asked.

"Feel what?" She was scaring me now.

She shook her head. "Nothing. Never mind. It just felt like someone was watching us."

I felt the hairs stand on my neck and arms. I looked around but saw nothing.

"Come on!" she excitedly pulled on my arm, "Let's go plant rutabagas!"

She recovered and we had a great time planting the seeds and chattering about all things a pre-teen girl chatters about: boys, girly gossip, school, but I felt a churning in the pit of my stomach. She had never reacted like that before and it had me worried.

By early afternoon, the incident was forgotten and we stood back to survey our handiwork. As long as you used the term, straight rows, loosely, we did a very good job. Corrie made little signs for each of the rows. She really wanted to try some corn so we put in the token row of corn. Wally was our brute force digging the trenches, removing errant rocks, and raking the rows.

"How long till we can eat this stuff?" she asked scrunching her nose against the bright sun.

"Oh, we have a while but in the meantime, we have to keep it weed-free and watered. You helping on that part?" I teased.

She put her hands on her hips and playfully frowned, "You know there are child labor laws, right?"

I coolly replied, "Then I guess I'll have the rutabagas all to myself!"

"I'm helping! I'm helping!" she squealed.

I put my arm around her shoulders and led her into the house leaving poor Wally to put our tools away.

As I reached into the cupboard to get her a glass for lemonade, I noticed something on the counter. I picked it up and looked at it. It was a square of chocolate.

"This yours?" I turned to her.

She shook her head, "What is it?"

"Just a square of chocolate," I answered absently. I shrugged and threw it away.

Wally came in wiping the sweat from his brow and I put a glass of lemonade in his hand before he could say anything.

Something was bothering me, something niggled and worried at my gut but I couldn't identify it.

Once we were cleaned up, Corrie wanted to know if we could go for a walk in the mountains. She shared our love for the mountains and often wanted to go with us. She and Spirit would explore, wander (though not too far) and romp in the wide-open balds. Sometimes, when it was just the three of us, I would feel that little tug in my heart that perhaps, maybe, possibly, I might want a child of my own…someday. I always nipped that little ridiculousness in the bud!

That night after my shower, I went into the kitchen for a drink of water. I reached into the cupboard for a glass and stopped mid-reach. There on the counter was the square of chocolate.

Have you ever had such a feeling of dread you felt like you had to pee?

Chapter Two

On Saturday morning, Wally was up and dressed, ready to go to yard sales. I wasn't much in the mood but I dutifully got dressed and followed him to the car.

"You okay?" he asked as he put the key in the ignition.

"What? Yeah, yeah, I'm fine," I said as I buckled my seat belt.

"You sure? If you don't want to go, we don't have to," he said with that sweetness that was all Wally.

I smiled at him, "No, I do want to go. I think I'm just...I don't know. You ever have one of those days when nothing's wrong but it feels wrong?"

He smiled back, "Yeah. Hate those days. Well, let's see if we can get you out of your funk."

We went to several sales and I honestly could not get into it. I didn't see anything I wanted or even interested me. I felt like I was looking for something in particular but had no idea what that might be. Wally got all excited about a set of kayaks but I put the kibosh on that. Eventually, he suggested we just go for a drive and relax for a while. That sounded good to me. My head felt crowded with thoughts, jam-packed full, but I couldn't identify any of them. I kept seeing that one square of chocolate on the counter.

"Did you see some chocolate on the kitchen counter the other day?" I suddenly broke the silence.

"Umm...yeah. I ate it," he said sheepishly.

I turned in my seat to look at him. "You ate it?"

"I wasn't supposed to?" he asked.

"No, I mean, yeah, I mean, I don't know. Where did it come from?" I was confused, getting all tangled up in sensations, thoughts, and feelings.

"Red? What's going on? Was it rat poison or something?" he asked as his brow furrowed.

"I don't know. I'm being honest, I just don't know," I answered.

"You've acted weird ever since we planted the garden," he stated.

"I know!" I acknowledged that fact. "And I don't know why. Something just feels off."

We rode in silence for a while. We were out in the country. Suburban sprawl was replaced with family farms. Cattle stood grazing in fields, tractors were planting crops, it was just a beautiful early spring morning.

"I want to go home," I said abruptly.

"Okay," he said without argument. He turned around and headed back to town. Neither of us said a word the rest of the way home.

As we pulled into the lane, we saw the familiar beat-up red bike. Corrie sat on the front steps with her chin resting on her cupped hands. She brightened when she saw us and skipped down the walkway to greet us.

"I thought you guys were never going to get home!" she stated rather firmly.

"What are you doing here? Aren't you supposed to be in school?" I asked as I put an arm around her shoulder.

"It's Saturday, Skunk. Geez," she laughed.

"Oh, good! Free child labor all day!" Wally teased. Corrie wrinkled her nose at him and stuck out her tongue.

We went into the house and I poured apple juice all around. As Corrie began to drink hers, she stopped and cocked her head.

"What?" I asked.

"That thing again," she said.

"What thing?" I felt my heart speed up a notch.

"Someone is watching us!" she whispered.

"Who?" Wally and I asked in unison.

Corrie rolled her eyes, "Duh! I don't know. You see anybody standing around?"

We all jumped a little when we heard the front door open. Miss Vera breezed into the kitchen. She had a tray of her famous cinnamon rolls.

We broke out in laughter. Miss Vera stopped mid-stride, "What?"

"Corrie is having feelings that someone is hanging around. I think we know now who it is," I chuckled having some fun at the expense of Corrie.

Miss Vera's eyes widened, "Oh? Who?"

We laughed that much harder and I managed to croak, "You!"

She shook her head and set the tray in the middle of the table. "I don't think so. I've been feeling the same way."

All of a sudden the laughter died.

"What do you mean you've been feeling the same way?" I asked, not sure at all I wanted to hear the answer.

She pursed her lips in thought. "I don't know how to describe it."

"You mean like someone's here but they're hiding?" Corrie suggested.

Miss Vera shot a look at Corrie, "Yes, dear, exactly like that."

That creepy-crawly feeling began to skitter up my spine.

"I think we might have visitors," I said with dejection. "I haven't felt quite right since last weekend."

"I can vouch for that," Wally chimed in. I shot him one of my death-ray glares. "What? Even you admitted you haven't been feeling like yourself."

"Anyway," I continued, "How do we get it to come out of hiding?"

Miss Vera went to the stove to put the tea kettle on. She stopped and stared at the counter. There sat a single square of chocolate. "What's this?"

I looked at Corrie in mock reprimand, "Corrie is trying to creep us out by leaving random chocolate laying around."

Corrie's eyes widened, "I did the what the what? I did not!"

"Come on, Corrie, I know it's you. The game is up," I chided her.

"Honest! It's not me!"

That skittering in my spine? Well, it was now in my brain. I looked at Miss Vera and Miss Vera looked at each of us. She picked up the chocolate and immediately dropped it.

"What's wrong?" I was feeling alarmed by now.

Instead of answering, she slowly turned in a circle. "Who are you?" she asked softly.

There was no response. "You're safe here," she added. "We want to help you but we need to know who you are."

"Look!" Corrie pointed to the backdoor window.

As we all whipped our heads in the direction of the window, we saw an elderly couple peering in. Just that quickly, they vanished.

Chapter Three

"I saw ghosts!" Corrie screamed with unbridled excitement.

"I did! I saw ghosts! They were ghosts, right Skunk? Oh my God! I can't believe it! I just looked up and there they were! You saw them, didn't you? I can't believe it! I saw for real ghosts!"

"Corrie, settle down," I scolded.

"You saw them though, right?" she was quite literally vibrating in her chair.

"Yes, we all saw them," I assured her. My mind began racing with the thought of a twelve-year-old girl telling everyone she saw, that she saw ghosts...at my house. Oh, this wasn't good, this wasn't good at all.

Miss Vera seemed shocked too. Wally was sitting in a trance-like state, white as a sheet of paper.

I turned to Corrie and held her by the shoulders, "Corrie, I need you to listen to me." Her eyes kept darting to the door. I guess she was hoping to catch another glimpse of the spectral visitors. "Corrie, calm down. Now listen, you can't go around yelling this all over town."

She cocked her head, "Why not? That was so cool! I've never seen ghosts before. I didn't even believe in ghosts but I saw them. I really saw them!"

"Corrie, I know you did but it's not...well...we just don't talk about it. People will think you're crazy," I tried to reason with her.

"I don't care what people think," she said firmly. What she said was true, she really didn't care what people thought or said. She had always been her own person.

Wally stirred a bit as if waking, "Corrie, these "ghosts" come to Red for help."

"You mean you've seen ghosts before?" she asked wide-eyed. I was shaking my head at Wally but he plowed ahead.

"Yes. Red is a very special type of person. Spirits come to her if they need help. She helps them and then they can go to Rest," he explained.

I felt sick to my stomach.

"What's Rest?" she asked.

"Well, Rest is where they go when their souls are finally at peace. Rest is good," he answered. "Red has a very special gift in that she can help them find Rest. That's pretty cool, isn't it?"

Corrie looked at me with a new respect. "How long you been seeing ghosts?"

I felt very uncomfortable discussing this part of my life so openly. It made me uncomfortable even around people who DID believe but even more so to those who didn't and I was downright terrified discussing it with a child.

Miss Vera saved me, "Corrie, describe exactly what you saw."

Corrie blinked, "Well, it was a man and a woman. They were kinda see-through so it was hard to see much but I think they were old people."

"Anything else?" she coaxed.

Corrie scrunched her nose in concentration, "There was something yellow. I couldn't see what it was but I could just see a yellow blob."

"Yellow blob?" I wasn't sure about that.

"Yeah, like maybe on the man's coat or something," she suggested.

"Is that what you two saw as well?" she asked Wally and me.

"Come to think of it, I did see a lighter area," Wally said softly.

"Yeah," I mused as I tried to reassemble the vision in my head, "They were dressed in what appeared to be old clothes. She had a scarf on her head."

We discussed the possibilities of the spirit's identity but the sight was so fleeting, so diaphanous, that it was hard to separate what we actually saw and what our brains were trying to fill in for a complete picture. After a while, we realized we were just saying the same things over and over. There were a few facts though that we could work with. One, my next mission had arrived. Two, unintentionally, a child had been dragged into my strange, dangerous world.

Corrie didn't want to go home. She didn't want to miss the chance of seeing 'her' ghosts again. I called Rosa and asked if Corrie could spend the night. I made some excuse about Wally wanting her to go hiking with us early Sunday morning. Rosa agreed and we had an overnight guest. I went into the living room and saw Corrie and Spirit curled up together sound asleep. It was late afternoon so I just let them sleep. I hoped that when Corrie woke, she would think it was all just part of a *super cool* dream. No such luck. Again, I tried to impress on her the importance of not talking about this with just anyone.

"So, it's a secret?" she asked.

"Well…no…not exactly." I had an idea, "It's a very special experience. It's the kind of thing people wouldn't understand anyway. If you go blabbing it around, it loses that specialness."

"Ohhhh…I get it," she said nodding her head. I sighed with a small degree of relief.

"Will we see them again?" she wanted to know.

"I don't know," I answered honestly, "But I'm thinking we will. They're here for a reason. It's our job to figure out what that reason is."

"Our? You mean, I get to help you?" the excitement was kicking in again.

"Maybe," I hesitated. I was never any good with kids. We were in deep doo-doo if Wally ever wanted a family. Mom material, I was not.

"Can't you just ask them what they want?" Out of the mouths of babes.

That night I tried to keep things as normal as possible as Miss Vera and I fixed the evening meal. She made meatloaf, mashed potatoes, green beans, and a lemon meringue pudding. As Corrie was taking her last bite of pudding, she wrinkled her brow, "Hey! Look! There was a piece of chocolate in the bottom of my pudding!"

Suddenly, it made sense. The chocolate was from the old couple. I believe they were leaving it for Corrie, not for me. Now, I did want to help. I did want to know more about them. I had great feelings of affection for them.

The next morning, we woke early. Corrie was up and dressed before Wally and I even wiped the sleep from our eyes. Spirit knew we were going somewhere. He was prancing and doing his famously, adorable wolf grin. Corrie was tying her sneakers. I hate morning people...even kids.

"Hey, why don't you and Corrie take Spirit out back?" I suggested.

"Come on, you two hellions," Wally smiled and the three of them headed to the backyard.

The kitchen was very quiet once they were gone. I didn't have much time.

"Hi. I'm Probably Magic. I think they call me Red Probably Magic in your world. I would very much like to help you if you need help, which I'm betting you do. I need you to show yourselves to me though. Are you here? Can you show me?" I said softly.

I watched as a shadow slid along the kitchen wall. It stopped at the table. I was holding my breath. Mist began to swirl lazily, twisting and turning upon itself. It began to take shape and there stood my ghosts. I smiled.

They seemed very nervous and afraid.

"It's okay. You're safe here. I will protect you with my life."

The couple began to cry silently. I could see the anguish in their faces.

"It's alright," I assured them. "I can help you."

The woman reached out her arms pleadingly. I felt ice in my veins, my mouth dried, and my stomach suddenly felt it was full of boulders. 556324 was tattooed on the inside of her right arm. I felt the tears spring into my eyes. If ever I wanted to hug someone out of compassion, it was now. I deduced from her tattoo that the yellowish stain on the man's coat was the Star of David.

I heard a gunshot and glass exploding in the living room. I ran toward the sound. There was no broken glass, no bullet hole. Just like the other time when Wally and I were canoodling on the sofa. It had to be related to the old couple though.

I went back into the kitchen but they were gone. A square of chocolate lay at my place at the table.

Chapter Four

Wally and Corrie stomped into the kitchen with Spirit on their heels. They were play arguing about something and Spirit was trying his best to join in the fun.

"It's still going to be cold up there, Corrie, go get your insulated vest out of the coat closet," I told her.

When she left the room, I moved in close to Wally. "I was able to communicate with our guests," I whispered.

"Oh, yeah? Did you find out who they are?" he asked as he kissed me on the cheek.

"No, not really but I saw something on the woman's arm. She had a tattoo of numbers," I said and I was surprised I felt tears coming on again. What was up with that?

"Numbers? What kind of numbers?" he reached in the cupboard for some water bottles to fill.

"I don't know, like maybe, you know, the concentration camps?"

Wally whirled around to face me, "As in Holocaust concentration camps?"

"I think so and I think what you and Corrie were seeing on the man's coat is the Star of David."

"Wow," he sighed. "What else? Did they tell you what they wanted?"

"No. I heard what sounded like someone shooting out the front window. When I went in there though everything was fine. Remember that time last winter when we heard that shot? By the time I got back in here, they were gone," I could not understand this overwhelming sadness.

"Who was gone?" Corrie asked.

"No one," I said and busied myself with stuffing some snacks into a backpack.

We hiked and played in the lingering snow. The air was crisp and smelled of spring. The runoff was feeding the creeks and waterfalls enough that I felt the need to caution Corrie about getting too close. We sat beneath a lone Hemlock in the middle of a bald and marveled at the green mist of new leaf buds just waiting on that one special sunbeam to make them burst forth.

Corrie ran to us and flopped on the cold, wet grass. Her face was flushed and a sheen of sweat glistened in the sun.

"I'm hot!" she exclaimed as she reached to take off her insulated vest.

"Don't take that off. It's still too cool up here and you'll get a chill," I told her. Wow! When did I turn into my mom?

Corrie sat up and began pulling blades of grass. Spirit stuck his nose close to see if she found anything interesting.

"You think those old people had kids?" she asked.

"I really don't know anything about them, Sweetie," I said.

"How do you think they died?"

"I don't know. Sometimes we don't know."

"They seemed real nice. I didn't feel scared at all," she announced. "Old people are nice, aren't they?"

"Hey, who said we were playing twenty questions?" Wally laughed at her.

Corrie shrugged her shoulders.

"You think they'll be back?" she couldn't help herself.

"The possibility is high, I would say," Wally chimed in.

"How's come they were dressed weird?"

"I think that's enough questions for now. We should head back and get you cleaned up so you can head home," I said as I began picking up our trash and putting it in the trash bag we always brought with us. "You have school tomorrow."

"Yuck," she said shaking her head.

Oh, but if life could stay so simple! We hiked back to the car with Spirit running ahead trying to get Corrie to follow him. Instead, she slipped her hand into Wally's and walked silently with him. I had begun to think she looked at Wally as a father figure. Her father had been killed in a car accident the day they brought her home from the hospital as a newborn. As for my opinion, she couldn't find a better stand-in than my Wally. He was so good with kids. He had several brothers and sisters, so I guess he was used to being around them. Not like me, an only child of parents that barely knew I existed. There was that melancholy again. This was so not me and I had a feeling it had to do with the old couple.

Once we got Corrie headed home, which I might add, I experienced the power of a pouting child, we settled in for a late bite of dinner. I looked at Wally across the table whose grilled cheese sandwich was oozing melted cheese all over his chin. Suddenly, I felt all warm and fuzzy toward him. I looked at my beautiful ring and the love I felt for him was immeasurable. This was the man I wanted to spend the rest of my life with. This was the man I wanted to have a real home with, real children, not rented ones.

"What? I still got cheese on my face?" he asked.

I smiled tenderly and shook my head.

"What's going on, Red?" he asked suspiciously.

I gave a little laugh, "Oh, I was just thinking how much I love you. I mean, I really, really love you. Not just a little bit but with everything in me. Every cell, every breath, every beat of my heart."

"Now you're scaring me. You okay?" He looked like he was about to bolt for the door.

I stood up and walked to his side of the table. I wiggled onto his lap and put my arms around him. I leaned in and kissed him. A full-on kiss. I felt all melty inside. He put a hand on my bottom and the other on my belly. I felt a tickle deep inside.

I'm not exactly sure what happened after that, the next thing I knew we were kissing, disrobing, and making our way to my bedroom. He put me against the wall and I instinctively let him hold my hips. We were panting, breathing in precious air, yet, resenting the fact we had to stop long enough to take a breath.

He lay me on the bed and kissed my neck. He moved to the tender area of my collarbone. He lay a hand on my breast and gently massaged it. I felt rivers of emotion, sensations, and desire flow through me to my very womanhood. I gasped as he undid my jeans and began to slide them off. I felt his fingers tremble, I felt his heart racing, I felt his erection straining against his jeans.

"What if they're hiding from someone?" I panted.

"What?" he panted in return.

"It just occurred to me that we keep hearing those gunshots. I thought they looked afraid, didn't you?"

Wally stopped and raised above me, "What in the hell are you talking about?"

"The old couple. It's like a puzzle. He's got the Star of David on his coat. She has a numbered tattoo on her arm. I'm sure they're from the Holocaust so what if they feel they still have to hide from the Nazis?"

Wally stared at me for a moment. "Okay, I'm going to point something out here. We were on our way to making love, which I remind you is the very first time, and while we're working toward that, quite romantically, I might add, you're thinking about the Holocaust? Does anything look wrong to you with that picture?"

It dawned on me. Yeah, I could see what was wrong with that picture. "Oh, I am so sorry! You're right, of course. I just get obsessed with these missions. I'm sorry. Where were we? I promise I'll pay attention." I wiggled my butt to get back in position.

Wally stared at me a few more seconds then rolled off me and started to laugh.

"What's so funny? Continue," I felt kind of insulted if you want to know the truth.

He kissed me then flopped over to his side, "Give me just a minute and we'll talk about the old couple. You know what, though? I could never, ever, love another woman like I love you. Everyone else would be just too damned boring!"

I have to admit, that was pretty funny. I reached up and kissed him too.

"Why don't you go make us some tea and we'll talk about the old couple. I have a couple of ideas too," he said as he playfully slapped my bottom.

As I finished putting myself back together, I looked at him, "I really am sorry."

"No, you aren't but that's what I love about you," he smiled.

He's so patient with me.

Chapter Five

We sat at the kitchen table at 1:00 in the morning discussing our thoughts and trying to decide on a plan of action. I wasn't sure how we would go about finding out who the couple was but a part of me felt it was crucial. I thought it strange they couldn't seem to communicate in the usual way but Wally suggested it might be they didn't speak English. That was a thought.

"I'll get hold of our friend, Cannon Reed, at the university to see if he has any ideas on how to track down people who lived through the Holocaust," Wally said. He had his laptop open and was researching anything he could find about the Holocaust. I was playing with my cup of hot tea. We all must contribute, you know.

"The thing is, how do we know they lived through it?" I asked.

"Well, they're dead now," he pointed out. He leaned back in his chair and stretched his back. "What really puzzles me is what are they wanting you to help them with? I mean, you can't undo history, you can't bring back the six million Jews executed, you can't make everything all better, so, what do they want?"

I chewed on my lower lip, which I'm prone to do when I'm deep in thought, "I think the first thing we need to do is find out who they are. Maybe once we find that out, other clues will begin to emerge."

"I'm tired," he said yawning.

"Me too," I admitted.

"We'll start fresh in the morning," he said snapping his laptop closed. "You talk to Miss Vera today?"

I hadn't and I realized I hadn't since our meatloaf dinner. "No, I haven't," I said sheepishly. "Surely if she needed something she would let us know. Maybe she's just been as busy as we've been."

"Doing what?"

"I don't know, whatever people like her do. How would I know?" I said defensively.

Wally looked at me, "We'll check on her first thing in the morning, okay?"

"Okay. Well, g'night," I said shutting off lights and checking the locked doors.

Wally stood for a few seconds in the dark.

"Did you need me to turn the light back on?"

He shook his head, "Night, my love. See ya in the morning."

We went to our respective rooms. I could smell his scent on my pillow, the covers were rumpled, and I could feel him panting as we prepared to make love. Well, crap. I blew that all to hell. What was wrong with me?

Spirit climbed on the bed and sprawled out.

"Hey, bud, move over. You can't take up the whole bed," I scolded him.

He stretched out even more and raised his head to look at me mockingly.

"Oh! I see what your sneaky butt is doing. Well, it won't work. Move over, Fido."

As it was, I lay in the dark staring at the ceiling. Maybe Spirit was right, maybe I should finish what I started with

Wally. The thing was, I just didn't feel...what was I supposed to feel? On TV there was a frantic desire to join, to explore, to become sweaty and exhausted and finish in exhilaration. Was that part of me broken?

I woke as thunder rumbled and a brief flash of lightning illuminated the dim bedroom. I heard the rain hit the window with lazy, intermittent *pat-pat-pats*. I got out of bed and looked out the window. Heavy gun-metal gray clouds moved over the mountain tops. The clouds lit up like an old-fashioned flash camera. I softly padded into the kitchen to put the tea kettle on. I liked the stillness of morning and there was something cozy and assuring in having this time to myself.

After I fixed my tea, I sat at the table looking over the notes we took earlier. I looked at it as a puzzle. Each piece had a place and was interlocked into another piece. I felt something was staring me in the face but I just couldn't focus enough to realize its meaning. Suddenly, the hairs on the back of my neck raised and goosebumps prickled my arms. The tattoo. She had one but I hadn't noticed him having one. Could it have been covered by his coat sleeve?

If Mrs. Ghost had one and Mr. Ghost didn't, could that mean she somehow survived but he didn't? How could I find out anything about them when I didn't know who they were? I felt two pieces of the puzzle click into place. I reached for Wally's laptop and slid it in front of me. I opened it and began to research the meaning of the tattoo. Exhausted and frustrated, I turned the stove off and went back to bed in hopes of getting an hour or two more sleep.

After finally getting just a few hours of restless sleep, I woke to sunshine streaming in my window and voices. I lay very still just listening. I hoped I wasn't hearing conversations of the dead again. No, wait. That was Corrie!

I tiptoed over to the window and peeked out. She was sitting in the garden pulling weeds just chattering away. Who was she talking to?

I slipped on a pair of jeans and a Led Zepplin t-shirt and went out barefoot. It was still pretty chilly in the mornings but hearing Corrie talk to no one was a bit worrisome. She looked up.

"Awwww…you scared her away!" she pouted.

"Scared who away?" I asked afraid of the answer.

"The old lady," Corrie answered as though I was a moron.

"What old lady?" I didn't like the direction this was going. Sure, Corrie saw or didn't see the old couple in the window but now she was out here in the garden just chattering away with 'the old lady'. I did not like this at all. OR could this help our investigation? Part of me felt guilty for knowingly, intentionally dragging a child into this mess but obviously, the old lady felt more comfortable talking to a little girl than the grown-up woman who could actually help her.

"So, what were you talking about?" I asked casually, "And why are you here so early?"

"I worried about the rutabagas and wanted to pull the weeds around them. Look! They've got little tiny green leaves! That's good, isn't it?" she beamed at me.

"Don't you have school today?" I asked.

"Yeah, but I thought I'd catch the bus here, or," she looked up through her eyelashes, "*You* could take me to school."

"Ha, ha, ha, you're a little sneak," I laughed. "Does Rosa know you're here?"

"I don't know, she was still asleep when I left," she replied.

"Okay, tell you what. I'll go call your mom and let her know aliens didn't abduct you. You get cleaned up and I'll take you to school," how could I turn down those big blue eyes and those cute freckles that seemed to glow when she smiled.

"'Kay!" she jumped up and ran into the house.

I followed her and noticed the comical surprise on Wally's face when she burst through the door. "Got to take Stink-O to school," I said with a chuckle. "I'll explain later."

He continued to get his cereal bowl down, "You have breakfast yet?"

Corrie shook her head.

"Come on, you can have Cap'n Crunch with me. Be quick about it though," Wally said as he poured milk on two bowls of sugary sin.

"Great, get her on a sugar high right before school." All I could do was envision a home with a white picket fence and children around a noisy table. I hoped my biological clock didn't drown out my common sense completely.

I called Rosa and let her know her wayward child was with us and I would take her to school. We would definitely have a little chat about appropriate times to visit.

"Can Spirit come with us?" she asked while wrestling with the wolf.

So, it was, my nice calm morning was blown clean out of the water and found Wally, me, Corrie, and a two hundred eighty-pound Wolf going to John K. Carson Middle School.

Life was messy, chaotic, and unpredictable, but like me, it was never boring.

On the way home, Wally gave me a sidelong glance and grinned, "You gonna tell me what that was all about?"

I didn't want to answer because I wasn't sure myself at this point but, after all, he did share his coveted Cap'n Crunch with Corrie. I guess he deserved some kind of an answer.

I related the chain of events as best I could and I could see he was really concentrating on trying to follow.

"So, the old woman is showing herself to Corrie but not to us," he summed it up pretty well.

"Yeah, apparently," I agreed.

"Did the old woman happen to give her a name?"

"Umm…I didn't ask."

"Did said old woman happen to give us a clue as to what they want?"

"Yeah, I didn't ask that either."

Wally slowly nodded his head.

"I was still trying to wake up!" I said defensively. "I wasn't thinking about giving a twelve-year-old girl the third degree!"

Wally stared straight ahead. He wasn't mad or anything, just lost in thought. However, I sat there mad at myself for not having been on the ball enough to ask some vital questions. I wasn't sure I wanted a kid in on this adventure. Who knew where it would take us? What if they were hiding from Brendore? How would I protect her?

Chapter Six

When we pulled into our drive, Wally got out and headed towards Miss Vera's house, I headed toward mine but I quickly adjusted and followed him like a little lost puppy. Where was my mind?

Wally knocked on the door. No answer. He knocked again and we heard a shuffling on the other side. The door opened just a crack. I stepped back when I saw watery blue eyes and frizzy, unkempt hair peer through.

"Morning, Miss Vera," Wally said carefully.

"What do you want?" she asked with a throaty croak.

"Are you okay?" Wally was edging his foot closer to the opening. I felt fear start at my toes and slow crawl up my spine. "Can we come in?"

Miss Vera sighed heavily and opened the door a little wider. She shrugged and turned away.

We stepped into her kitchen and I know my gasp was audible. Dishes filled the sink. Crumbs, dried liquid, and half-made meals sat on the counter. Something had spilled on the floor. I knew this because I stepped in it and it nearly pulled my shoe off. What was wrong with this picture? EVERYTHING!

I went to her and led her to a kitchen chair. "Miss Vera? Are you sick? Why didn't you let us know?"

She looked at me as though she just didn't have the energy to answer. "I'm fine."

Wally glared at her, "You aren't fine. What's going on?"

"I don't know. I think I'm just going through a blue time. People do that, you know, they just feel sad for no reason then they perk right up," she snapped.

I didn't know what to say. I'd never seen her like this! The world was going crazy! Little girls were speaking to ghosts, old friends were acting strange, rutabagas were growing too fast. It was spinning too fast; I couldn't make sense of it. Then a thought that was barely more than a whisper marched forward.

"Miss Vera, Corrie was out in the garden talking to the old woman we saw in the window last week," I began.

Miss Vera looked at me.

"I've been feeling sad and tired. Is that what you're feeling?" I asked. "No reason, just sad and tired."

Miss Vera slowly nodded her head.

"I think it may be the old couple making us feel like this," I just threw it out there. It would either fly or sink like a stone.

"Why would that…" her eyes widened. "Do you think?"

I nodded my head, "I think they are projecting on us. Whatever it was that happened to them, I think it so filled them with sadness that they are projecting that sadness on us."

"Then we have to help them!" she wiped tears from her eyes.

"I agree," I said as I lay my hand over hers just as she had done to me countless times when I was at the end of my rope. "I don't think they mean any harm; this is just what they know. Sadness and fear."

Wally stood behind her and wrapped his arms around her. He lay his cheek on top of her head and closed his eyes. It was so loving, I felt tears puddle my eyes.

"Good heavens! Look at me! I'm a mess!" she cried.

"Shhhh...it's okay. We'll work together. We'll make it all better as long as we're together," I said as I patted and gently squeezed her hand.

Wally finally broke his embrace and sat beside his friend, "I have an appointment to talk to Professor Reed today. It feels like we've been burning rubber with engines racing but not getting anywhere at this point. We need a starting point."

Miss Vera nodded, "Do we know *anything* about them?"

I chewed my lower lip, "Well, we know they are a couple..." Wally rolled his eyes. "No! Wait, hear me out. We've never had a couple before. Could it be they generate twice the energy? That's why so many of us are feeling this...this...melancholy? All except, Corrie. She seems to like them and they seem to like her. Because she's a child? Maybe they had children and that's why the woman can relate to her more than us."

"I hate to say this, cause I don't want you getting a big head or anything, but you just might be on to something," Wally said with a smirk.

"Maybe if I tried to summon them. Maybe I could talk to them," I suggested.

"Or maybe, you could talk to the person they seem most comfortable talking with and find out what she knows." Wally was accusing me, I just knew it, he was accusing me because of this morning. For heaven's sake, I was just waking up! I'd like to see how alert and clear thinking he was if he woke up to someone talking outside his window!

I just glared at him. Miss Vera smiled. We got a smile out of her!

"I love you two so much," she said wistfully. "I just don't know what I'd do without you."

"We're not going anywhere, Miss Vera. You're stuck with us like dog poo on a shoe," I assured her.

She stood, "I'm going to shoo you guys off so I can make myself decent and get this place cleaned up. I just don't...How did I let it get this way?"

We left her as she began stacking dishes and running hot soapy water. I'm glad she was feeling better but I vowed to keep a very close eye on her.

Wally went to his appointment with Professor Reed to see how we might be able to track our visitors and learn a little more about them.

My phone rang and assuming it was Wally, I answered, "Yeah?"

"Probably?" Rosa asked.

"Oh, Rosa! Hi! We got Corrie to school in plenty of time," I offered before she could ask,

"Oh Good, but I didn't have any doubts you would," she said. "I wondered if I could talk to you a minute?"

"Sure! What's up?"

"It's about Corrie," she said and I felt the bottom drop out of my stomach.

"Okay, sure, what's going on with the little goony head now?" I was trying to keep it light because I was pretty sure I knew what was coming.

"I don't know how to say this," she hesitated.

"Well, just say it and we'll go from there," I suggested to her.

"I feel stupid. In my mind, I had it all planned out but now that I'm about to say it out loud, I feel...it sounds..."

"Rosa. Look at all we've been through. You can't say anything in this world that would shock, disappoint, or anger me. We're more than friends, we're family and you can say anything to family. Right?"

She still hesitated, "I'm worried about Corrie. I always dreaded the thought that the accident would have effects on her later as she matured but I pretended that wasn't going to happen. No chance of that happening. After all, lots of people have brain injuries and do just fine. Don't they? Right?"

"I doubt she's having effects of her brain injury, Rosa, but tell me what's going on," I said and I was surprised I could get enough breath to get the words out.

Her voice lowered to a whisper, "She's got an imaginary friend."

"A what?"

"I hear her in her room talking to someone. When I look, there's no one there," she said softly.

"Rosa, I can hardly hear you. Corrie's talking to someone? Look, how about I come over and we can talk about it over a cup of coffee. That sound good?" I asked. This wasn't a conversation I wanted to have over the phone.

I heard a rubbing noise and I figured she was nodding her head. "I'm on my way."

Rosa must have been looking out the window because I'd barely cleared the first step when the door opened.

"Hey," I greeted her. I took her hand as I led her inside the house, "Look, we'll talk it out and figure out the best solution, okay?"

She poured me a cup of coffee; she knew I didn't drink coffee but that showed me just how distracted she was.

"Rosa, I'm sure you're worried about nothing," I began.

"I don't think so. Something is different about her. Do you think she's unhappy about something? I asked her and she said she couldn't tell me. What kind of secret is she guarding? You don't think she's…you know…experimenting with drugs, or something, do you?"

Her concern slammed into me, I was the one Corrie was protecting and no child should ever have to protect an adult from their parent. "Tell me from the beginning."

She took a moment to get her thoughts together, "Well, a couple of weeks ago, when she came home from your house, she was different. She's a happy kid but this was something more than that. It was just different. Then, as I was putting away laundry, I heard her talking. I thought that was a good thing! Maybe she had a friend, finally. It hasn't been easy for her to make friends, you know. She's always been somewhat older than her years. She just never got into the whole doll phase, or dress up or anything that most little girls get into, so, I was happy to hear her talking to someone. I thought they were talking on the phone."

"That sounds innocent enough," I interjected.

"Yeah, except when I took her clean clothes in to put them away, she didn't have her phone and there wasn't anyone in the room," she said.

"Well, what kinds of things was she saying?" I asked.

"I don't know. I couldn't hear exactly what she was saying. Anyway, I asked her who she was talking to and she said, Vesta," she looked at me with worried eyes.

"Who's Vesta?" I asked.

"I don't know. I asked her but she just said Vesta was her friend. I asked her if Vesta was in her class and she said no. When I pressed her, she just said never mind and clammed up. What's going on with her, Probably, do you know? Has she talked to you?"

I had a split second to make a decision and I just hoped my instinct made the right one.

"Rosa, you know about me helping spirits, right? Remember the old magician and how I had to go into the Realms to free the souls Brendore was keeping imprisoned?" She nodded.

"Well, a couple of weeks ago, we think we have a couple of spirits; a husband and wife apparently, who need my help. The thing is, they seem to be afraid of something. They won't show themselves to me but they seem to have taken a liking to Corrie," I explained as gently as I could.

"Oh no! Probably, no!" she cried.

I hadn't expected her to react with such panic, "Rosa! Rosa, they seem like a sweet, elderly couple. I don't get any feelings of harm from them. They're just afraid. I'm sure they have no plans to harm any of us."

"But you said they wouldn't show themselves to you. How would you know?" Rosa's voice was shaking.

"Well, they have actually shown themselves for just a fraction of a second but I can feel them and I don't feel a threat from them whatsoever. Corrie happened to be there when they appeared but it was just a nano-second, I promise. We think they may have been victims in the Holocaust. We just don't know much about them at this point," I assured her. Then I quickly added, "They're harmless. They need help and they're scared and confused and for whatever reason, seem to have taken a liking to Corrie."

"Who are they and what do they want? What if they want Corrie to join them?"

"I don't think we have to worry about that. All I know is that from what little I have seen of them; they seem to be from the Holocaust period. We're trying to find out more. Wally is with a friend of his who is an archaeology professor at the university to see if we can fill in some of the blanks. This guy is a whiz at research, I'm sure he'll turn up something," I was talking fast.

"I don't like it. She's much too young to be exposed to such things," Rosa said through tight lips. "I think that perhaps it best she not come over to visit until you get this resolved, or whatever it is that you do."

"Rosa-"

"I'd like you to leave now," she said standing up and essentially walking me to the door.

I sat in my car shaking. I felt I had made a colossal mistake. It was only a gateway to more trouble. Corrie would not take kindly to being restricted from seeing Wally and me.

I started the car and drove home. I couldn't tell you if I stopped at traffic lights, if I nearly ran over unsuspecting pedestrians, or even if I stayed in my lane. I was on autopilot because my mind was firmly fixed on the old couple and what it meant that they related more to Corrie than to me.

Chapter Seven

Wally was home and I stomped through the door in a foul black mood. I'm pretty sure there was a thundercloud over my head. He opened his mouth to say something and then snapped it shut.

"I hope your morning was better than mine!" I barked.

"Red, what on earth happened? Are you okay?" he asked as he rushed to me.

"Okay? Well, I suppose I'm okay considering I've gotten Corrie involved in something she has no business being involved with. I'm okay considering ghosts are now going to...Notice I said the words *'going to'* Corrie's home to talk to her. I'm okay considering Rosa is angry with me and won't let Corrie come to visit here anymore because it isn't *safe*!" I stopped to take a deep breath, "Sure! I'm just peachy-keen-o!" and then I collapsed into a puddle of tears.

"Hey, hey, I'm on your side, remember?" he said as he gathered me into his arms. "Calm down and tell me what happened. We can fix it. We can fix anything together, remember?"

I told him what I knew and rather than making me feel better, I felt like the world was sitting on my chest, wiggling its butt right on my heart.

He led me to the sofa and sat me down. I felt like I weighed five hundred pounds. He offered me a glass of lemonade. I shook my head.

"Okay, I agree, it most likely is dangerous for Corrie to be in this mess but you didn't get her involved in anything. We have to figure out why they are seeking her out and then maybe we can reason with them and direct them back to you. Rosa is being protective of her daughter, you can't blame her for that," he said reasonably.

"I would NEVER allow a hair on her head to be harmed!" I protested.

"Red, it's her daughter. Remember the beginning of Corrie's life? I have no doubt Rosa has made it her life's mission to protect her daughter above all else. We have to respect that," he said.

I knew he was right but I kept seeing Rosa's face. Chiseled from granite, her eyes shuddered from me, and her escorting me to the door. It cut deep.

"Wally, the longer this goes on, I'm starting to hate that couple. Sweet, old couple, my auntie's ass. They've affected Miss Vera, me, Corrie, and who knows who else. What if they're just puppets from Brendore?" I was starting to feel even more angry. Livid as a matter of fact. Blinding, seeing red mad!

Wally thought very carefully about speaking next, "Red. Honey, I understand how you must be feeling but when you calm down enough to think this through, I think you'll begin to see a picture start to form."

"Calm down? You're telling me to calm down?" I shouted.

"No! No, I'm not telling you to calm down. I'm telling you *when* you calm down, you'll start to see a clearer picture. I already do and I don't have much more information than you do," he said quickly.

"Oh? Did you find out anything useful today?" I asked between sniffs and outbursts.

"Okay, Cannon said if he had the inmate number, he might be able to look it up in forensic records. He explained that the Nazis assigned numbers instead of names to dehumanize the prisoners. He thought it interesting that the woman would have the number and not the man. It was a horrible time; Red. Human cruelty knew no bounds. The general population had absolutely no idea what was going on. In fact, much of the German army didn't know the extent of what was going on. It was Hitler's own inner circle that was killing the Jewish population. Hitler wanted the perfect society so he granted psychopathic doctors to experiment on the prisoners. It was beyond horrible. I can understand why our couple feels they have to hide," he was speaking calmly but I could see the anguish in his eyes. "Perhaps if we reassured them, they are safe here, they will leave Corrie alone and come to us."

Made sense. Of course, I'd read about the Holocaust in school. We had some generic discussions about it but then we moved on to more current events and it was tucked away and forgotten. For this couple, it never ended. Their moving on meant death.

"556324," I whispered.

"What?" Wally asked.

"Her tattoo. That was the number. It was on the inside of her forearm. I didn't notice one on him but I thought it was because he had that coat on. That number is branded on my brain as surely as it was on her flesh. 556324." I couldn't seem to get my voice to rise above a whisper. "I think her name may be Vesta."

"How did you come by that. Did she talk to you finally?" he asked as though I was hiding important information from him.

I shook my head, "Rosa said Corrie's invisible friend's name is Vesta."

Wally pursed his lips, his forehead furrowed right up to the hairline, "Okay, we've got something to work with. Would you say Miss Vera is about the same age as our Vesta?"

"Mmmm...I don't know how old Miss Vera is and I can tell Vesta was old beyond her years. She most likely didn't have an easy life but I'd say it's a good possibility. What are you thinking?"

"What if we had Miss Vera talk to her? You know, kind of coax them out of hiding?"

The more I thought about it, the more it sounded like a good idea. The two women would have more in common, perhaps Vesta *would* feel more comfortable. "Let's go ask her."

Miss Vera. God bless her sweet little pea pickin' heart. I would challenge anyone on the face of the earth to find another human being more compassionate than Miss Vera. I would swear she was God's grandma and that's why He is so loving, kind, and compassionate.

"I'll try anything to help those poor souls," she said when we posed the question to her.

We filled her in on everything this day had presented to us. She kept nodding as she took it all in. When we had exhausted everything we could think of, theories included, she nodded one last time.

"I think it's worth a try," she said at last. "As far as Corrie goes, let me take a go at Rosa. I'll see if maybe I can put her mind at ease. Don't you kids worry about a thing. That being said, maybe Rosa is right for the time being. I would feel better if we excluded her until we learn more about the situation and what is involved."

It was wonderful having Miss Vera back, the real Miss Vera. For the first time since this whole ordeal started, I felt hopeful. Miss Vera suggested we get some rest tonight and she would come over in the morning and see what or who she could scare up. It was time for a little ghostly chat.

Wally and I walked back to my cottage holding hands. I felt closer to him than I had ever felt in my life with anyone. I grabbed hold of the doorknob and the door swung open.

There stood Aunt Jo. Uh-oh, that was never a good sign.

"Huh. I didn't see your broom parked outside," I huffed.

"Hardy Har. Can't an auntie come visit her favorite niece without some snarky comment?" she shot back.

"Umm…well, a normal aunt and a normal niece maybe but you? Me? I don't think so. Whenever you show up, trouble isn't far behind," I said as I breezed past her pulling Wally behind me.

"Well, then I guess you're not interested in my information about a certain ghost couple," she said inspecting her fingernails.

I whirled around, "Information? What information?"

She gave me a mysterious smile and walked into the kitchen to find the coffee can that I kept just for her. She began the ritual of making a pot of coffee and rummaged through the cabinets while it brewed.

"You got any of those little gingerbread cookies?" she asked over her shoulder.

"If you want a cookie, you have to tell me what you know," I said slyly.

She laughed, "Oh, I don't really want a cookie. The coffee will be fine."

"Aunt Jo!" my voice held a warning and she knew it.

"Okay! Don't get your panties in a twist!" she fixed her cup and sat at the table putting her heavy boots on the next chair.

I swiped them off the chair and sat down, staring at her.

"What do you know about the old couple," I said through clenched teeth.

"I know their names are Vesta and Jacob Krause. I know they were rounded up by Nazi soldiers and shot in the head," she said smugly.

"Shot in the head?" I felt every ounce of aggravation drain out of me.

Aunt Jo sat up straight in her chair, "I also know what they need from you."

"What?" Wally and I asked in unison.

"They want you to kill Adolf Hitler," she said and leaned back in her chair smiling in satisfaction.

Well, it wouldn't have taken more than the whisper of a butterfly wing to knock me off my chair.

Chapter Eight

I blinked at her in confusion, "But Hitler is long since dead!"

"They don't know that," Aunt Jo pointed out.

"So, if I tell them he can no longer hurt them, they'll just go on to Rest?" I asked hopefully. Something told me it wasn't going to be that easy though. No, there was something else going on here. Something that made them keep their heart and soul bound to the land of the living. Something only the living could give them. I had long since learned nothing in the spirit world was easy. The frustrations of needing to do something and being unable to do it for themselves were always at the root of their unrest.

"See, I don't think that's it," I said already lost in thought. "While I understand their situation was desperate, there has to be something that was even more important than their death. There is something that they so wanted that even death didn't stop them from… What?"

"How would we find out what it was in their personal life?" Wally asked. "We have their names, what if we tried to find the family?"

"I vote for tracking down Hitler. That sounds like more fun," Aunt Jo giggled.

I rolled my eyes at her, "Fun for who?"

She shrugged her shoulders at me.

"Well, one thing is for sure, we aren't going to get anywhere until we can convince them to come out of hiding," I reached for a peach from the fruit bowl in the middle of the table. Just as I was getting ready to take a satisfying bite out of the juicy bit of deliciousness, I had a thought. "I need to somehow convince Rosa to let me talk to Corrie."

"You think that's a good idea?" Wally asked with worry lines wrinkling his brow.

"Yeah, I do. Rosa said Corrie was having *conversations* with Vesta. She may have told Corrie things she wouldn't tell us," I explained.

"That makes sense but Rosa's mama bear is coming out. She'll do anything to protect Corrie," Aunt Jo pointed out.

"What if I talked to her while Rosa was there? You know, right in the same room with us?" I suggested.

"Worth a try," Wally said shrugging his shoulders. "What's the worst that can happen? She gonna shoot you?"

We all kind of chuckled but truth be known, no matter how much Rosa and I loved and respected each other when it came to Corrie, all bets were off.

"Look, all I know is that Hitler is long gone, and once I tell Vesta and Jacob that, it's not going to be over. They're still going to be hanging around. We have to know what they *really* want us to do," I argued.

Everyone nodded except Aunt Jo. "You take the fun out of everything," she pouted.

"Wah," I snapped.

The next morning, after tossing and turning and finally running Spirit out of bed in frustration, I was pretty sure how I wanted to approach Rosa. After all, it wasn't like she had never seen the kind of life I was given. Granted, it was only the slightest peek but enough for her to know I was different and why. I simply needed to reassure her that her daughter would not be making any trips to the Realms nor would she be fighting demons. All I wanted was to have a conversation with her. A fact-finding mission, if you will.

Wally fixed breakfast for me and we talked about reassuring things I should say. He didn't seem to think tact was my strong point. I honestly think he was more concerned about what would come out of my mouth than the actual conversation. Aunt Jo stomped into the kitchen and without saying a word started making a pot of coffee. She clearly wasn't a morning person. Corrie was a different kind of kid. She was just as brutally honest and opinionated as I was. It was all these other people on the sidelines that caused concern.

I heard Rosa's phone ring. My hands were shaking. *Do it right, do it right*, I chanted in my mind.

"Hello, Probably," she answered with an unaccustomed flatness.

"Hey, Rosa," I greeted cheerfully.

"What do you want?"

"Oh, just checking in to make sure my two best gals are doing okay," I said lamely. Oh, that didn't sound suspicious at all.

Silence on her end.

"Okay, Rosa, here's the deal. You know I help spirits find Rest. You know I'll go to any length to help them find that Rest," I mentally slapped my forehead. Why did I put it like that? I hurried on, "Well, there's this older couple who were…they were in the Holocaust. Jewish couple, I believe and they're afraid so they've been hiding."

"You're not getting Corrie involved in this, Probably."

"I agree! Oh, boy! Do I ever agree!" I said perhaps a little too loudly. "See, the thing is, apparently, they feel safe with Corrie, that's why they're talking to her. I mean, can you blame them? You do know about the Holocaust, right? Of course, you do, I mean, who doesn't, right? Anyway, apparently, they want me to murder Hitler…"

"You think you're helping your case and you aren't," she said tightly.

"Okay, I can see where you think I'm going to have Corrie help me commit murder but that's not it! All I need is to know what Mr. and Mrs. ummm…I forget their last names. Their first names are Vesta and Jacob. They seem to be very sweet and I really don't see them harming Corrie, they just need help and don't know how to ask for it," I was pretty pleased with myself.

"I have to go now. It's time to go pick up my groceries before Corrie gets home from school. Leave Corrie out of this, Probably and I don't mean to sound harsh because I dearly love you and Wally and the others, but I love my daughter more. Please do not call again until this is over," she said. I heard the dial tone.

I just stood there staring at my phone. "She hung up on me," I said with hurt feelings.

"We'll figure something out, Red," Wally said rubbing my back.

I wasn't listening. "I could go to her school! I'll try to get her alone and talk to her there!"

Aunt Jo pursed her lips, "I could be wrong but I think there's a law against stalking little girls."

I shot her a withering glare, "I'm not stalking her. I just want to talk to her."

"Mama said no. Mama trumps whack job. You keep it up and Mama's going to open a can of whup-ass on you," Aunt Jo warned.

I slumped in the kitchen chair discouraged, frustrated, and hurt that Rosa didn't trust me. How could she not trust me?

Wally looked at his watch, "Oh, I have to go. I have an appointment with Professor Reed. Red, promise me you won't do anything stupid until I get back. Who knows what kind of information Cannon can give us? Just be patient, okay?"

"Wait, did you just use the words stupid and patient in the same conversation?" I said incredulously.

"You know what I meant. I have to go. Stay put. Promise me you will stay right here," he pointed his finger at me.

I mocked him by sticking out my tongue. "I'll try not to do anything 'stupid' as you put it. I will not leave the house."

He kissed me on the tip of my nose, "I love you, whack job."

After Wally left, Aunt Jo was laughing as she retrieved her little red scooter and headed down the road.

I really, really wanted to get Corrie alone. I just know she knew what Vesta and Jacob really wanted.

The house was too quiet and the conversations in my head were too loud. I decided I needed my mountains. Things always made more sense when I went to the mountains. I called to Spirit and got my car keys. I walked out to the garage and put him in the backseat.

Pssst!

I stopped and looked around. Living at the foot of the mountains in Colorado, one learned to look for things like rattlesnakes curled up in the most surprising places. I didn't find any unwelcome slithery things.

Pssst!

I was puzzled. Did one of the tires have a small leak? I checked to make sure I didn't have a tire going flat.

"Skunk! Geeze! You'd make a rotten secret agent!" I heard a stage whisper.

I felt my eyes open to nearly popping out of my head, "Corrie! What are you doing here? You're going to get in so much trouble!"

She looked both ways and then slid into the garage going to the back where it was deeply shadowed. "I don't have much time," she said.

"You're supposed to be in school," I stated the obvious. No wonder she thought I was dumb. I thought I was dumb. She had that effect on me. She was the type of person who gave the appearance she was always in control of her surroundings and herself. That was so not me!

"Yeah, and as far as you know, I am. Look, I got a bathroom pass. For all my teachers know, I'm puking my brains out, that's why I've been gone so long. I heard you talking to Mom. She's so annoying! I'm not a baby anymore!"

"Corrie, she loves you and just wants to protect you," I said kicking into my version of mom mode.

"Shut up and listen," she said irritably. "Vesta and Jacob are scared that they'll be hunted down again. I explained to them that the war was over, we liberated the prisoners who remained, and Hitler had the decency to kill himself in his bunker. Like the monster he was, he crawled back underground to do the deed. I even showed them my history book."

Corrie never ceased to amaze me. Why hadn't I thought of showing them proof that they needn't be afraid of persecution anymore?

"I need to know what they want me to do," I said.

"I don't know that but I have someone I want you to meet," she said. "It's okay. You can trust Skunk. She'll be able to help you. She's kinda goofy but she'll help."

I watched in amazement as first Jacob then Vesta manifested. They still looked very nervous.

"It's okay, guys. Give her a chance," Corrie encouraged them. "I have to get back to school but I'll try to come back later."

"Corrie, your mom said no," I said though secretly I would love it if she did come back. I gave her a quick hug. "I'll take you back. It'll be faster."

Corrie shook her head, "No one can see me with you, Skunk."

"I'll let you out in the back lot. Can you sneak back in?" I suggested.

Corrie gave me an eye roll, "Hello? I made it out and over here with no one seeing me."

"Oh, yeah, right," I mumbled. "Okay, let's go. Vesta, I'll be right back. You guys stay here, okay?"

They nodded. Jacob was nervously fingering the brim of his hat. Vesta was half hiding behind her husband. I put Corrie in the car and took her back to school. I think I'd make a great secret agent!

Chapter Nine

When I returned home after dropping Corrie off at school and after quite the stern talking to about skipping school (*Don't do that anymore, okay?*), I looked for my scaredy-cat ghosts. They were nowhere to be seen. I swear, this cat and mouse, hide and seek, was exhausting. There they are! Nope, they're gone again. Oh, here, stay here. Crap, they disappeared again. Back and forth, back and forth.

Miss Vera came over with cherry turnovers and tiny lemon poppyseed muffins. I followed her into the house and we sat in my kitchen. It never escaped my attention that my kitchen was the most used room in the house and yet I did very little cooking. It just seemed to have morphed into a type of base camp.

"You're out and about early this morning," she commented as she took a bite of the turnover. "Did I see Corrie? Isn't she in school?"

I snared a lemon poppyseed muffin with a mental note to check my teeth for stray seeds, "Yeah. Little stinker ran away from school."

"Oh, dear! That's not going to make Rosa happy!"

I kind of laughed and I don't know why. "She 'brought', so to speak, the old couple with her."

"So, you got to talk to them at last?"

"Not exactly. I had to take Corrie back to school and when I returned, they were gone again," I said as I went to the stove to put the tea kettle on.

"That's a shame," she commiserated with me.

"What about you, Miss Vera? You have any ideas?" I asked noting the frustration in my question.

"Well, I did talk to an acquaintance of mine. A Dr. Leslie Turnbow," she said hesitantly.

"And?"

"And I'm not sure we want to enlist the good doctor's help," she said softly.

"Why not?" I couldn't help but feel we were starting the I've Got A Secret games again.

"Probably, you're looking at this as a mission like all the others. This isn't like all the others. This is stirring up memories, people's lives, it's so horribly painful. Perhaps Vesta and Jacob can sense you don't really understand them. Perhaps they feel you can't appreciate just what that period of time was like for them," she said and I couldn't decide if she was scolding me or not. I definitely felt scolded.

"It was a war, Miss Vera. Terrible, ugly, hurtful things happen in every war. There is no such thing as a neat and tidy war where everyone goes home with a participation trophy," I argued in my defense.

Miss Vera shook her head, "No, sweetie. While you are right about the characteristics of war, this one was much worse, much more destructive, cruel beyond what you could possibly understand. It calls for compassion, respect, and patience. This was a war that changed the world. A war that must not be repeated at all costs. Yet, as you are illustrating and it isn't your fault, it has been downplayed, the history of it and what led up to it, is being forgotten."

"I don't know how to respond to that," I said. "How can I understand something I know very little about. I only know what I was taught."

"Therein lies the problem," she sighed.

"I'd still like to talk to the doctor friend of yours. Perhaps she can educate me," I tried to sound willing to try anything.

"I will try to set a time then," she spoke with a great deal of reluctance and I just didn't understand.

Wally walked in the door and plopped down at the table.

"Well?" I asked a little more sharply than I intended.

"Not a whole lot of the kind of help we need," he said as he took a cherry turnover.

I sighed heavily.

"Well, Red, you have to understand, the Jews were stripped of any humanity. They were nothing more than victims of medical experiments, a workforce where dogs were treated better than them. They didn't keep records, or artifacts, or family information. They were numbers. Nothing more than numbers until they died of starvation, sickness, or exhaustion. Professor Reed tried and he did teach me a lot that isn't talked about in schools but nothing that would lead us in any kind of direction of finding out what our guests want of us," he said. The turnover lay untouched in front of him.

"Would everyone quit telling me what I don't understand and just tell me what the hell I'm supposed to do?" the frustration broke free like Old Faithful and just as hot and forceful.

Wally looked at me, got up, and went into the living room. I may have possibly crossed some line.

"I'll talk to Dr. Turnbow and set something up," Miss Vera repeated.

All I could do was nod; I didn't trust my mouth.

She left and I noticed her gait was as though she carried the weight of the world. I hoped this Leslie could shed some light on the subject. I just knew it was affecting all of us. I didn't know what to do about it. Wally said he was going to the library to read up on the Holocaust and perhaps learn more about the area, the people, their lives.

Around six in the evening, there was a knock on the door. I answered it and there stood a tiny man in a navy-blue suit and bright red bowtie. He wore thick, wire-rimmed glasses that magnified watery blue eyes. A black bowler set atop his head which I suspected was bald.

"May I help you?" I asked and I couldn't help looking down at him. Was I supposed to kneel so I could be closer to his height?

"Yes. Are you Probably Magic?" he asked squinting up at me.

"I am. And you are?"

"I'm Dr. Leslie Turnbow," he said with great authority.

"You're Dr. *Leslie* Turnbow?"

"I am and if you have any cute albeit insulting remarks about my name, I would request you keep them to yourself. I can't imagine you are original enough to come up with something I haven't already heard," he snapped.

I wanted to laugh. I mean, I really, really wanted to laugh. Here was this tiny little man that couldn't be more than 4'8", with a girl's name, a bowler atop his head, and the bright red bowtie. He was glaring at me. Kind of like a rabid gerbil.

"I just have one question," I said as seriously as I could muster.

"You may ask your question," he said tightly.

"What's your middle name?"

He stared at me for a few seconds before saying, "Carroll."

That did it. In my defense, I've often laughed at the most inappropriate times. I don't know if it's a nervous habit or some broken part of my social graces in my brain. He turned to walk away.

"No! Wait!" I cried, "I'm sorry. I truly am sorry. Please, come in. If anyone knows what a name can do to a person, I'm the poster child."

"What do you mean?" he asked.

"You know, because of my name," I explained.

"What's wrong with your name?"

"You know. My name is Prob…never mind. Please, come in," my laughter was at least under control.

He was hesitant and he kept eyeing me like he expected me to pounce on him but he did come in. I showed him to the living room and let him pick a seat. I asked him if he would like a cup of tea and he said that would be lovely.

I used my kitchen time to get myself under control. I don't mean to be rude but like I said, inappropriate, broken wires, damaged brain, yada, yada, yada.

When we settled, I asked him, "What can I do for you?"

"I assure you, Miss, there is nothing you can do for me. I'm here for you. The lovely Mrs. Silverstein asked me to be your consultant," he sniffed.

"Mrs. Silverstein?" Then I remembered I had heard that name attached to Miss Vera, "Oh, Miss Vera! Yes, she did mention you. I didn't know she was going to have you actually come. Okay, we're on the same page now."

"I highly doubt we are but I'm here. I understand you have a rather frustrating case. Mrs. Silverstein, or *Miss Vera* as you call her, called on me to help you understand Vesta and Jacob Krause."

"You know them?" I asked.

"No. Not directly but I am the Secretary Treasurer of Realm Four," he explained.

"The who of the what in where?" I felt my stomach drop.

"I am the record keeper of all wayward spirits. Most I can point the way for them to go but there are some stubborn souls who absolutely refuse to conclude their journey until something has been resolved," he explained.

I felt my mouth hanging open like a Neanderthal. I snapped it shut. "So, in your record-keeping, you know what this sweet old couple wants?"

"No," he answered.

"I'm confused," I admitted.

He slid off the couch and walked to where I was sitting in the armchair. He started to reach for my forehead and I jerked my head back. "Hey! There will be no touching!"

"Do you want the answers you seek or not?" he barked.

"Yes, but do you have to do that whole handsy touchy thing?" I whined.

"Yes."

"I don't like people touching me, especially strangers," I warned him.

He sighed heavily and said, "Very well then. Good day, Miss."

He walked to the door and opened it.

"Wait! You were going to tell me what Mr. and Mrs. Krause wanted from me!"

He turned to look at me with one hand still grasping the doorknob, "No, I could not possibly know what they want from you. I was only going to show you their moments before death but you have to use your own deductions as to what the answer is that you seek."

"Like a vision?" I asked. I was familiar with visions. They didn't scare me like they used to.

"It isn't a vision exactly," he said as he searched for the right words.

"Please, come back. I'll do what you want," I pleaded with him.

I really wished Wally, Miss Vera, or even Aunt Jo was here. I felt uncomfortable with this odd little man.

"Mr. Turnbow-"

"Doctor," he corrected me.

"Sorry. Dr. Turnbow, I've been in some pretty dangerous situations since I've taken on this mantle of whatever it is. I'm a little paranoid," that was as close to an apology as I could come up with.

He hesitated.

"Please, I know there's a whole hell of a lot I don't know about all this but they seem like such good people, I really want to help them," I was begging now.

"Very well. Under one condition," he said still not moving from the door.

"What condition?" I asked cautiously.

"You will do exactly as I say. No insults, snarky comments, or quitting until we are finished. You'll want to end it, you won't like what you're going to see but you must press on to understand," he said staring at me directly in the eye.

"Okay, I'll try," I promised.

"I don't want you to try. I want your word," he was strongarming me and that part of me that wouldn't allow anyone to push me around was rearing its ugly head.

"I promise," I said trying to beat back the panic.

He had me sit on the sofa. He stood in front of me taking off his glasses. He put his index finger on the bridge of my nose between my eyes and began to slowly make circles. It felt kind of good actually.

"Look into my eyes," he instructed.

His faded blue eyes began to sparkle. Like a kaleidoscope made of glitter. I was so mesmerized by them I couldn't have looked away if I wanted to. Suddenly, I felt as though I was falling. I was falling into darkness and I couldn't catch myself. There was nothing to hang onto. Nothing but the kaleidoscope eyes.

Chapter Ten

It was very cold and dark. I was somewhere but I didn't know where. I felt around in the dark until I found a door. I slowly opened it a crack and peeked out. It was a hallway with dim lights barely illuminating the worn carpet runner. I stepped out. Slowly I made my way toward a brighter light but not much brighter. I saw an old woman sitting in a straight back chair, head bent, shoulders indicating she was doing something with her hands. I crept closer not wanting to frighten her or me.

Vesta tied off the last knot and broke the thread with her teeth. She raised her head and listened. I wasn't even breathing. Did she know I was standing right behind her?

She heard footsteps. I could hear them too. I waited to see what would happen next.

"Mama! I'm home!" I heard a male voice announce.

She lay her sewing aside and stood to greet him. He gave her a peck on the cheek and asked what was for supper. Like a gut punch, I realized I was witnessing the final hours of Jacob and Vesta's lives.

"I was so lucky today!" she said with great excitement, "Toadee had extra turnips and four potatoes. I used a bone broth and made us a fine stew today."

Jacob boyishly smacked his lips and smiled, "I can hardly wait. Let me go wash up first, Mama."

As they sat eating their meager meal, Vesta told him she had finally finished the Wedding Quilt. "I don't know when I'll be able to ship it though. With this war, everything is out of kilter. It feels like she's halfway around the world!"

Jacob laughed, "She IS halfway around the world, Mama! Leah will appreciate it when she gets it. Have you heard from her lately?"

I mentally made a note of the name Leah.

"Oh, she is very busy. Her husband is in banking and works long hours. Poor Leah must tend to baby Maria while Elizabeth works in a factory. She says Michigan is helping with the war effort but I don't know what that means. How I wish I could be with her to help."

Okay, who is Elizabeth? Another daughter, granddaughter?

Jacob patted her hand. He looked troubled but he did not show it to his wife.

"How was work today?" she asked as she finished sopping the stew with bread.

"My bones say it was a long day," he smiled. "My soul says it was a tiring day. I'm not as young as I used to be."

"Oh, Jacob, you've worked so hard all our lives. I wish you could not work and we would be okay," she sighed.

"Don't you worry, Mama, I will always provide and care for you," he assured her. "Let's say our evening prayers and go to bed. I just want to hold you close."

She blushed and hurried to straighten the kitchen. When she sat down in the living room, Jacob lit a candle and his head bowed in servitude. He looked up as she settled in her chair.

He smiled and they said in unison, holding hands, heads bowed.

In the name of Adonai the God of Israel
May the Angel Michael be at my right,
And the Angel Gabriel be at my left,
And in front of me the Angel Uriel.
And behind me the Angel Raphael...

And above my head the Sh'khinah.

With reverence, they blew out the candle together and walked to the bedroom.

Once they had gone to bed, I used this time to do some good old-fashioned snooping. I examined the quilt Vesta had been working on. It was breathtakingly beautiful. I fingered the material and the knots made by a skilled embroidery seamstress. I could feel little things in each of the squares. Like something had been inserted between the two layers of fabric.

I read the family tree of names and noticed the dates. This quilt was nearly one hundred years old! I moved on to the tiny kitchen that still smelled of turnips and bone broth. I saw a newspaper wrapped around a small crock of butter. I carefully removed the newspaper and flattened it on the postage-stamp-sized counter. Apparently, I was in Klamry, Poland. The date at the top of the paper read, April 11, 1943. The paper was full of stories from the war with Germany. Heil, Hitler! Fear, like a snake curling around my veins, made me tremble. Vesta and Jacob and millions of Jews rose each morning in fear and if they were lucky enough, lay their head down at night on a pillow of fear. I felt the heaviness, the oppressive weight of living such a life. Nothing whatsoever was said though about concentration camps except for one lone article. It was about the work camps in which the captured Americans were held.

I heard a stirring and only then noticed the gray and pink sky of dawn. I didn't know if they could see me or not, so I hid around a corner in a pantry.

Vesta rose before Jacob. She fixed a breakfast of oatmeal and the last slice of bread. For his lunch, she gave him the leftover bone broth stew. She bit her lower lip trying to think of what else she could add to his lunch.

She rummaged in the icebox and found a pear. It was bruised on one side and a bit on the soft side. She put a chunk of cheese wrapped in cheesecloth in the metal lunchbox and stood back satisfied.

Jacob came into the kitchen and wished her good morning. She reached up and touched the yellow Star of David on his jacket. He took her hand in his and kissed it.

"If you go out, be very careful," he warned. "This war has made our day-to-day lives very unpredictable. Always be aware."

"I will Papa. You be careful too!" she said.

Such were their lives. While they praised God and gave thanks for each day they were gifted, still, the worry and constant vigilance stole the color from the days, brightness from the smiles, and openness from their faces. Life had become a palette of grays, browns, and slate blue. I felt tears sting my eyes.

Vesta said a prayer of protection as her husband left for work. She returned to the wedding quilt and looked at it with longing.

Vesta added a special touch of her own. She had written a letter to Leah. She hoped it conveyed hope in these uncertain times and peace should she not see tomorrow's sunrise.

She carefully wrapped the quilt and hid it in a secret cupboard in the tiny dining room. She hoped it would be safe and if anything should happen to her and Jacob, that it would find its way to Leah. One just never knew. One just kept the faith in God and trusted He knew best.

Another day passed while she busied herself scurrying to the market to see what food she could afford for the evening meal. I followed her every step of the way. She found a piece of chocolate that was marked into four squares! I saw her hesitate. I saw the concentration in her eyes as she calculated her purchases as opposed to the amount of money in her apron pocket. I saw her take a deep breath, close her eyes for a second, and then hand the merchant some change for the chocolate. She bought a small chicken, two potatoes, and compensated by not buying bread. I saw her hesitate by the bread vendor but she set her jaw and kept going. She smiled all the way home.

I was still shaken to the core by the simple means of pleasure. Chocolate! I thought about the times I was in the grocery store and never even hesitated buying candy to enjoy later. To her, she had to make a decision and decide what to sacrifice to have one small piece of chocolate. Now, it made sense why she wanted Corrie to have a square of chocolate. It represented happiness to her.

"Sister Vesta!" she heard her name. I snapped my head around to see a middle-aged woman with two small children hurrying to Vesta.

"Vesta, I have made bread today!" she announced. "For some reason, it made too many loaves. I would like to gift you two loaves of bread."

Vesta raised her eyes and thanked God for the provisions but I could tell she felt bad taking two loaves, a very generous gesture to be sure when so many were trying to eke out enough for families with children. I saw her face as she knew she must pay for the loaves. That was the only way she could accept them in good conscience. I saw her grudgingly finger the chocolate. Still, this was an opportunity to have not only bread but *fresh* bread!

"I will trade you two squares of chocolate for the two loaves," she said before she lost her nerve.

"Chocolate? Where did you come by chocolate? That would be a wonderful treat for the children!" the woman glowed with anticipation.

Vesta handed her two squares of chocolate and took the two loaves of bread. She thanked the woman, whose name I learned was Esther, profusely but her heart begrudged the two squares of chocolate, I could tell. At least she and Jacob could have one square each.

That evening felt festive. They enjoyed the chicken, boiled potatoes, and fresh bread with butter fresh from the churn. Jacob told funny stories from his work and they laughed together. After the meal, Vesta presented Jacob with the chocolate. His eyes became wide as he stared in disbelief.

"Vesta! We cannot afford such luxuries!" he chastised her.

"No! I had four squares but Esther offered me two loaves of fresh bread for two squares of chocolate. So, see? I got everything we needed for our evening meal and was able to treat us. You work so hard, Jacob. You deserve a treat now and then," she spoke but she could feel the tears in her eyes.

"You are a good woman, Vesta. I'm sorry I reacted so badly. It's just times are so..."

"I know. It will make them even sweeter on the tongue," she said softly and handed him the full two squares of chocolate.

He handed her one square and they took the smallest of nibbles from the delicacy and then wrapped them to save for later. They would make it last as long as possible.

They said their evening prayers and Vesta silently asked for forgiveness for begrudging Esther the chocolate in turn for the bread. They went to bed and Jacob extinguished the lamp next to the bed and then turned to his wife. It was almost like when they were first married. She slept in contentment while the war raged outside their door but she was at peace with the man who loved her.

I felt like a peeping Tom but the love between this husband and wife was so beautiful, so giving, so complete, I wondered if when the time came for Wally and me to lay in our marriage bed, we would have such fullness and contentment.

The next morning, they went through their morning ritual. She hid a tiny piece of chocolate in Jacob's lunch pail and giggled when she thought of him finding it tucked away. Jacob kissed her and once again urged her to be safe and smiling, he turned to her and said, "And no extra surprises today, my love. You'll have me expecting such extravagances all the time!" She laughed with him.

I found myself smiling from ear to ear with them. They were old people yet, here they were as happy and in love as a young newly married couple. My heart felt it would burst with the love I shared with them.

As he reached for the front door it suddenly flew open knocking him backward from the impact. Vesta didn't even have time to react. The German soldiers swarmed into the tiny apartment and grabbed Vesta by the arm.

I screamed in shock and fright!

"We'll go with you!" Jacob shouted, "Please! Don't hurt her!"

Vesta's face was distorted with terror. Jacob began to quietly cry as the soldiers roughly pushed them out into the street.

I followed them out, powerless to stop what I was sure was unfolding. On either side of the street Jews were lined up single file. I saw a young family with an infant daughter and a five-year-old son. I saw an old man who moved slowly, bent with twisted bones and aching feet. I saw a young woman who still had the best of her life ahead of her. Esther stood shivering with her two children trying to hide behind her skirts. They were all wild-eyed with fear, trembling under the unblinking eyes of the soldiers.

Jacob reached for Vesta's hand. He could feel her quaking. He squeezed it tighter.

"I love you, Vesta Krause. You have been the love of my life and all any man could ask for in a wife," he said softly. "Remember the chocolate. No matter what happens next, think of the joy of the chocolate."

She looked at him and nodded and closed her eyes.

I heard the click behind their heads.

"Schießen!" (Shoot)

I screamed and screamed until my stomach hurt and my chest felt like it was in a vise. Through the blur of tears and rage, I saw the soldiers light up cigarettes and laugh as they looked at the dead bodies lying in the street. One soldier took the toe of his boot and nudged the little boy. The boy rolled away from his mother. They began to remove jewelry, gold teeth, and wallets from the murdered victims. I collapsed and continued to scream obscenities at them. Then there was blackness. I could no longer see the carnage. I could no longer hear the cruel laughter. I could no longer feel anything. I was numb with shock and desperation.

Chapter Eleven

As though dawn was trying to peek through my eyelids, I slowly began to focus. There was a great weight within my body. My throat burned from the screaming. My eyes felt swollen and raw.

"Open your eyes," I heard. I was terrified to open them. What if a Nazi soldier was standing over me to finish me off?

"Remember, you are an observer. Nothing can hurt you here," the voice said softly.

I opened my eyes and I wished I had kept them closed. I saw a mound of dead bodies. Children, babies, men, women, elderly, and those who should have had their whole lives ahead of them. The sky was gray and a cold wind blew. Stray snowflakes fell leaving a dusting on the bodies. I walked toward the mound when I noticed movement. I stood staring at the place that moved and I heard a moan. Someone was alive! I ran to help.

"You cannot interfere," the voice warned.

I felt the tears slide down my nose. I watched as first, a hand appeared, then an arm.

"Please, please, try harder!" I yelled.

It seemed to take forever before I saw a woman struggle against the weight of the bodies as she emerged. Exhausted, she rolled down the mound and lay on the cold, frozen ground. I ran to her.

"Vesta!" I screamed.

The woman was covered in blood. She had no coat and only one shoe. My heart broke. She staggered to her feet and put a hand to her head. She used the hem of her skirt to wipe the blood from her eyes. I could see a gash above her right ear. The bullet had torn through the flesh but missed entering the skull.

"Jacob?" she called but the only answer was birds screaming high above and the wind whistling through the open field. She knelt and cried.

"Please, help her!" I pleaded with the disembodied voice.

There was no answer. Vesta stood and walked woodenly away from the macabre mountain of the dead. I hurried to walk beside her. She stared straight ahead with unseeing eyes.

We walked until the gray sky began to turn into black sky devoid of stars or moonlight. Her skin glistened with ice. She was freezing to death and I could not help her. I couldn't quit crying as she stoically continued on stumbling once in a while but never did her eyes leave the straightforward course she was bound to.

We came to an abandoned farm. I prayed she would seek shelter and to my relief, she stopped and studied the farm. She turned and walked up the drive to the house. She knocked but, of course, there was no answer.

"Sarah?" she weakly called out. "Abraham?"

She tried the door and it easily swung open. The house had been ransacked but she didn't seem to notice. She went into a bedroom and searched the closet for warmer clothing. She lay them on the bed and went into the bathroom and began to wash the blood from her face and arms. Once she had cleaned herself as best she could, she returned to the bedroom and put on the warmer clothing. She seemed to have just noticed she only had one shoe. She broke down and cried. I cried with her. I wanted to hold her so badly I shook with frustration. I did though, I sat beside her and put my arms around her. She didn't know I did but I did. Finally, she found a pair of boots and though they were too big for her, she put on layers of socks and then the boots.

We then went into the kitchen. She found canned peaches, a small piece of ham in the fridge, and some apples. She stuffed the apples in her pockets and sat at the table and ate the peaches and ham. It was a very small meal but she couldn't eat all of it. She would take a bite and then rest. A bite, rest, and so on until she could eat no more. The cut on her head began to bleed again. She kept swiping the blood away, which was replaced by a new flow. She hunted through the cabinets and drawers until she found a dishtowel and wrapped it around her head. When she finished her meal, she sat at the table staring out the window. I don't know what she was thinking about but I was pretty sure it was about Jacob and all her neighbors and the little children. They were all dead. She survived. I'm sure she wondered why she survived.

She went into the living room and looked in an antique credenza and found a candle and a prayer book. She took it to the kitchen and sat back down, lit the candle, and began to pray. I have never had religious training. I don't know if she found comfort in it or not. I don't know what one is supposed to feel when appealing to their God. Right now, I felt God must be very cold and unforgiving. How could a deity wantonly let children die? How could it rip families apart and cause nearly unbearable suffering? These were my questions.

When she finished her prayers, she stood and put on a coat. The towel had soak through with her blood so she replaced it with a scarf. She went to the door to continue her journey but paused at the doorway and looked back at the empty house. I don't know if she could hear the wind whistle through the drafty windows or feel the chill of a house with no fire in the fireplace. I think, perhaps, she was saying goodbye.

We were back on the road. She had to be exhausted and drained but she walked on with me beside her. Soon, we came upon a sign that said Klamry. She was going home. Bless her heart, she was going home! What did she think she would find there? They were all gone. Given the farmhouse we were just in, I was sure the town had been ransacked as well. The soldiers taking family heirlooms, money, jewelry, art, silver, anything they could get their hands on that would be of value. I felt so much rage, I stumbled. I wanted to stop her from going into the apartment she shared with her husband. There would be nothing but sadness to greet her. I couldn't stop her though.

Instead of sneaking into town, staying within the shadows, checking for danger, she marched straight down the main street. I could feel her strength draining from her but she pressed on. When she got to the apartment building, she walked right in as though returning from the market. She went up the stairs and into her apartment. Chairs were overturned, the furniture had been ripped apart, the contents of kitchen cabinets emptied to the floor and drawers pulled out and tossed aside. She went to a bookcase and located a secret compartment. She pulled out a few pieces of jewelry and a quilt. The same one she had been working on when I first saw her. It was beautiful! She put it to her face and sniffed deeply. She began to cry. She heard a noise and quickly stuffed it back into the compartment.

A soldier appeared in the doorway. She stared straight at him. He spoke German but my head translated for me.

"What are you doing here?" he demanded.

She said nothing. Her breathing became labored as she struggled to find the strength to stand up to this murderer.

He grabbed her arm and yanked her down the stairs and roughly pushed her to the ground.

"This bullet will not miss you, you filthy Jew!" he shouted. He drew his weapon and held it to her head while holding her head steady by clenching her jaw with his other hand.

"Wait!"

I looked up to see a young soldier walking toward them. He looked down at Vesta and helped her up.

"What is your name?" he asked gruffly.

"Vesta Krause," she said with as much strength as she could muster.

"Are you a Jew?" he barked at her.

I saw her chin quiver but she bravely said, "Yes, sir."

The soldier turned her head and looked at her wound. He turned to his comrade and said with a sternness that spoke of rank and superiority, "She escaped the cleansing this morning. She has strength. We can put her to work in the laundry for the officer's barracks," he said.

The soldier nodded and roughly pulled her up by the arm and propelled her to a truck. He loaded her in the back and locked the door. I wasn't sure what was happening but at this moment it seemed as though this young soldier had saved an old woman's life. Still, I didn't know if I could trust him or not.

They drove her to a place called Auschwitz. It consisted of several buildings and barren lots surrounded with barbed wire. I was horrified at the condition of the prisoners. Mere skeletons with thin, splotched skin. They wore striped pajama-type uniforms that hung from their bones. Several were coughing deep and rattled as they tried to catch their breath. Some lay on the cold, frozen ground, too weak to stand for long periods. Yet, in those clouded eyes, I saw hope. I saw a smile or two. I saw the strength of their prayers. I wanted to save all of them. I understood why Jacob and Vesta first said they wanted me to murder Adolf Hitler.

I hurried to catch up with Vesta and her two captors as they entered a clapboard building. They took her name, checked her teeth, and told her to remove her clothes. She hesitated and the processing officer punched her in the back. She slowly began to remove all her clothes, her hands shaking so badly she could barely work the buttons. She stood before this group of men more vulnerable than she had ever been in her life. They took her to the showers and scrubbed her with a strong-smelling soap. Though she was trying to be courageous, tears slipped from eyes that kept staring straight ahead. They gave her a dress of coarse, scratchy material and allowed her to put her socks and boots back on. They grabbed her arm and held it firmly.

"556321," a clerk said without looking up. They took a tattoo needle and punched the number to the left inside forearm. She screamed in pain.

They marched her to another building full of soldiers who laughed and pointed and yelled at her. They deposited her in a laundry room with about eight other women, left, and locked the door behind them.

Day after day passed. Vesta worked twenty hours a day with only a slice of bread, one boiled egg, and a glass of water for her daily nutrition. She began to run a fever but she rose and washed uniforms and the filthy underwear of the Nazi soldiers. I'm not sure how long we were there but one night, Vesta lay on her bed saying her prayers softly in a sing-song voice. She turned her head and looked straight at me.

"Please, Leah must have the wedding quilt. Promise me," she whispered.

She could see me?

She was still staring at me but then I noticed…she was no longer breathing.

Chapter Twelve

I wanted to stay with her. I wanted to close her eyes and cover her. I lay across her and cried. I cried for all of them. I cried that a human was so capable, so willing, so comfortable to show such cruelty. These were good people! They loved, they raised families, they practiced their faith, hurting no one. They were gentle, honest, hard-working and their only crime was that they were of the Jewish faith.

"It's time to go," the voice said.

"Let me stay with her just five more minutes," I begged.

"She is not there any longer. She has left her body," the voice was gentle and sad.

I sat up and closed my eyes trying to mute the horror I had experienced.

When I opened my eyes, I was sitting in my living room with Dr. Turnbow. Wally was there too, and Miss Vera.

I felt I should say something but I didn't know what. Words seemed so insignificant at this point. I felt guilty that I should see such suffering, that I watched such a historical event and couldn't change it. I just plain didn't know what to say.

"Are you okay?" Wally asked.

I blinked at him. *No, I'm not okay. I will forever and ever carry this experience with me. I will always feel a piece of me die again and again every time it comes to mind. I will always search for a way to ensure it never happens again. It should have never happened in the first place.*

Why didn't someone stop it? Why didn't someone intervene and save those people? I nodded my head slowly.

"Thank you, Dr. Turnbow. I..." the words failed me. "I need to be alone now."

I got up and went into my bedroom. Spirit followed me. I lay on the bed trying to forget what I had seen, what I had felt. Spirit got on the bed and lay as close to me as he could. It was then I took two fistfuls of his fur and cried into his ruff.

The next morning, I awoke to sunshine. Even though it had been less than twenty-four hours since I had seen sunshine, it felt like years. It was cold and according to the weather forecast; snow was coming to the mountains before the end of day. I raked my hand through my long, unruly hair and shuffled to the kitchen to put water on for coffee. I found Miss Vera, Aunt Jo, and Wally waiting for me.

"What? This some kind of intervention or something?" I grumbled. "I'm fine, guys."

Aunt Jo set a cup in front of me.

"What's this?" I asked suspicious of any kindness from her.

"Just drink it," she ordered.

"I'm not even awake yet!" I whined.

"Good. Then you won't notice how awful it tastes," she said dryly.

Well, that didn't make me want to gulp it down. I sniffed it. I could smell ginger and lemon. It didn't smell bad. "Seriously, I'm fine. I don't need any hoodoo concoctions."

"Fine, then tell us what you saw yesterday," Wally piped up.

Well, that made the words curl up like paper in a flame.

"That's what I thought," Aunt Jo mumbled.

"I was afraid of this," Miss Vera shook her head. "I was so hoping we could find what we needed by other means. I would never call on Dr. Turnbow if there was another way."

"He's an odd little man, isn't he?" I observed.

Miss Vera humpfed, "If you'd seen what he's seen, you'd be a bit odd too."

"I'm sorry, Miss Vera. He really was very kind and as hard as it was, I'm glad he was here," and I was. Without thinking I picked up the cup and took a sip. It wasn't so bad! It made me think of the mountains where the wild strawberries grew. A tangy zip of moist earth, the crispness of the spray from a waterfall. It was quite good actually. I drank until it was gone. The coldness left my body and I was warm and at peace. One of these days I was going to learn to trust Aunt Jo's magic potions. Honestly, though, I think she was just a really good herbalist.

"Okay. Here is what I learned. Vesta and Jacob lived in a very small town called Klamry, Poland. They were part of the cleansing when the Germans invaded Poland. Everyone in Klamry was executed but somehow Vesta survived. At least for a short while, she did. She survived being shot in the head and then she survived a second attempt, saved when a German soldier stepped in on her behalf. She was tattooed, processed for Auschwitz concentration camp where she worked in the laundry until..." My mind went back to Vesta turning her head to look at me and asking me to promise to get the wedding quilt to her daughter. I felt tears threaten. "Until she died peacefully in her sleep."

"She sounds like a strong woman," Wally said.

"She was amazing," I agreed. "I also think the chocolate represents joy to her. The last thing her husband said to her was to remember the happiness of sharing the chocolate. He tried to give her a happy thought at the time they were shot. I got to see the wedding quilt. It's beautiful. All hand stitched with pink roses and garland around the edges. It was beautiful. The bad news is that she had hidden it in a secret cabinet in their apartment. I have no idea what became of it after she died."

"The what?" Wally put out a hand to stop me.

"The wedding quilt, the…" it suddenly dawned on me they had no idea about the wedding quilt. "It's the reason they're here. She made me promise I would get the wedding quilt to her daughter, Leah. It's beautiful, guys. It's nearly a hundred years of mothers passing it down to their daughters when they married."

"So, are you saying we have to somehow find this quilt and track down her daughter?" Wally asked.

"Yep, that pretty much sums it up," I said. "Is there any more of that tea?"

To my surprise, Aunt Jo made a second cup for me. Is it possible to overdose on magic potions?

We sat there with our thoughts. We now knew the mission. We now had absolutely, positively, no idea how to track a blanket that was over seventy years lost and we had no last name for the daughter, Leah.

I am not a technology guru. It took me a very long time to allow a cell phone in my life and then half the time I had no idea where it was. If not for Corrie, I wouldn't even know how to work the stupid thing. However, I had a daunting task ahead of me and I wondered if this social media phenomenon could help. I really needed Corrie's help and that meant I was going to have to reach out to Rosa again.

I practiced and practiced how to approach her. She made her feelings pretty clear the last time we talked about Corrie. I guess I could be sneaky and try to nab my young friend at school but that just seemed kind of creepy…even to me. I decided to talk to Wally about it.

He was flipping through the channels on the TV with Spirit sitting on the sofa next to him. They were sharing a bowl of popcorn. Heavily buttered I could see. Spirit had trouble with that stuff but Wally didn't seem to mind and Spirit certainly didn't mind if we had to open all the windows. Miss Vera was flipping through a magazine. I could hear Aunt Jo rummaging around in the kitchen with various clanks, paper rustling, cabinet doors opening and closing.

"Hey, can we talk?" I sat in the same chair I sat in when Dr. Turnbow led me through the vision.

"Sure! What's up?" Wally didn't take his eyes off the TV and Spirit didn't take his eyes off the popcorn.

"I need Corrie," I said simply. Well, that made Wally sit up straight and turn the TV off.

"You sure?" he asked doubtfully. "You remember last time, right?"

"Yeah, but I know more this time. It doesn't involve demons or the spirit world or anything like that. I just need to know how to use social media…unless you know how to do all that," I replied.

Wally gave a little laugh, "I know just enough to be dangerous. I have to admit that since we live the life we live, social media is kind of…what's the word I'm looking for…dumb? Boring? What are you thinking?"

"I don't know," I admitted, "But I can't help but wonder if we made a plea to find the daughter of Vesta and Jacob, maybe, somewhere, someone would recognize them."

Wally was nodding his head, "That could work."

"I just don't know how to do it," I said.

Miss Vera sighed heavily, "I'm afraid I'm no help in this new technology age."

Aunt Jo was deep in thought, "You got any donuts or muffins or anything sweet around here?"

I whipped my head toward Aunt Jo and burst out laughing. Aunt Jo. I hadn't even realized I had sunk back into the tarpit of despair and suddenly there was that figurative slap in the face that brought me back to the here and now. I couldn't help but to go to her and kiss the top of her aviator hat. Just that innocuous comment was enough to bring me to the mission at hand.

I went to get my cell phone to call Rosa one more time.

"Put it on speaker," Wally suggested.

"I don't have speaker," I said as I dialed the number.

"Everyone has speaker," Wally said as he reached for my phone. He poked at the phone and suddenly we could all hear the phone ringing.

"What do you want now?" Rosa answered the phone.

"Don't hang up!" I pleaded. "Please, just hear me out. I promise if you say no, I'll never bother you again."

"Okay, what?" there was an edge in Rosa's voice that told me she was already angry and closed off.

"You remember when Corrie fixed my phone and taught me how to use it?" I asked.

"What about it?" she replied.

"I need her expertise again," I said hoping I was showing her this had nothing to do with her little girl stalking spirits.

"With what?" she asked.

"I need to know how to do social media. I have no idea how all that stuff works and I know she's really good at all this…stuff. You can even sit right beside us so you can see exactly what she's doing," I was using the word 'stuff' an awful lot.

"Probably, I'm really uncomfortable with…"

"Honest, Rosa, nothing to do with the spirit world. Just some lessons about how to do things and then I'll send her home…or you can just take her straight home…you can stay right here with her," I was begging, not ashamed to admit that.

"Let me think about it," she hedged but at least she didn't say flat out no!

"Thank you, Rosa. When do you think you can give me an answer?" I pressed.

My only answer was the disconnected call.

"I don't know, that didn't sound all that promising," Aunt Jo piped up.

"But she didn't say 'no'!" I pointed out.

"Not in so many words, I guess," she conceded. "You might ought to have some donuts when she comes over or bake her a cake or something."

I rolled my eyes at her, "Would you get off the donut thing?"

"Tell me donuts don't sound good. Raspberry filled, cream-filled, lots of cinnamon…"

Miss Vera started laughing, "Come on, Jo, come home with me. We'll find something sweet for you."

As they left, Aunt Jo turned around and stuck her tongue out at me and then smugly followed Miss Vera to her back door. I stuck out my tongue too at her retreating back.

"I saw that!" she called back to me but I could hear the smile in her voice.

Chapter Thirteen

That night as Wally and I sat eating peach ice cream at the kitchen table, I noticed Wally was unusually quiet.

"What's the scoop, Scooby," I asked as I took a large spoonful into my mouth. Brain freeze! I moaned and held my head as the throbbing slammed into me.

Wally just laughed at my pain. He could be such a brat!

He purposely took a small bite and said, "I think the social media thing is a good idea but I wonder. What if someone responded, what would you say to them? Hold your tongue to the roof of your mouth."

I did and as the throbbing subsided, I thought about his question. "Well, I would tell them…that…" I couldn't just tell them that their relatives showed up as spirits and asked me to help them. I couldn't just talk about the wedding quilt because I didn't have it as proof. I realized I didn't have anything I could tell them.

"Well, I guess nothing," I said as I finished my treat.

"Yeah, maybe we should hold off on that part," he suggested. Now, see? That's why I needed this man in my life. He kept me from going off half-cocked on a mission.

"What would you suggest we do? We're not getting anywhere the way we're going," I felt the frustration build again. Why did this have to be so hard?

"I've been thinking about that. What if we contacted a museum?"

I blinked at him, "A museum? What museum?"

He shrugged, "I would say since the Holocaust was a major historical event, there's bound to be displays or even a whole museum dedicated to it."

"And then what?" I asked intrigued.

"I don't know, maybe ask them if they have a wedding quilt in storage somewhere?"

I thought about this. It made sense. Any reputable museum was bound to have a catalog of items in their possession. Would they know what a wedding quilt was though? What if they had hundreds of wedding quilts? Even if we did locate it, would they release it to us so we could send it on to the intended daughter?

Wally could see the onslaught of questions in my eyes. He put his hand over mine, "Let's just take it one step at a time. Okay?"

I nodded but my mind was still coming up with questions, flooding me with doubt and uncertainty.

Miss Vera knocked on the door as she opened it and stuck her head around the corner, "Oh good! You're still up!"

"Hey, Miss Vera, why are you up so late?" I asked.

"Oh, I just saw your lights on and thought I'd pop over," she smiled. "Oooo, is that peach ice cream?"

One of the things I learned about my dear friend was that she had a weakness for ice cream. She didn't even have a favorite, she loved it all! I retrieved the ice cream from the freezer and put three scoops in a bowl for her. Oh, what the hell, I put a couple more scoops in our bowls as well.

"We were talking about maybe contacting a Holocaust museum and see if they have a wedding quilt in their exhibitions," I summarized for her.

"'A' Holocaust museum?" she asked with the spoon stopping halfway to her mouth.

"An Holocaust museum?" thinking she was correcting my grammar, although it didn't sound right to my ears but what did I know?

She gave that little laugh I loved so much but usually meant she was laughing at me and not with me.

"Honey, there are museums and memorials all over the country. You need to pick one and start there. I would suggest the main museum in Washington D.C." she explained.

"Ah, okay. Would they have a complete catalog?" I asked.

"Most likely not. You're talking about six million murdered people…that we know about," she said. "However, I think it would be most conducive."

I looked at Wally and Spirit, "You boys feel up to a road trip?"

"Count me in!" Wally exclaimed with no hesitation whatsoever.

Spirit went to sit by Miss Vera.

"Traitor," I grumbled.

Miss Vera tried to hide a yawn behind her hand. It was late and I knew tomorrow was going to be extra busy.

"I don't know about anyone else but I'm ready for today to be over. I'm fried," I said.

I got some weak agreement from Wally and Miss Vera and we began getting ready to call it a day. I knew though, I wasn't going to sleep anytime soon. I had too many questions rolling around in my head like a roulette wheel.

Wally went on to bed and Spirit went to his corner in the living room. I turned off the lights and then I heard Spirit rustle from his bed.

"What is it, boy?" I whispered.

I looked in the direction his ears were pointed and saw a figure standing in the doorway of the kitchen.

"Hello, Vesta," I said softly. "I am so sorry for what you and Jacob endured. I don't know how I'll do it but I promise I will get the wedding quilt to Leah."

I saw her smile.

"Can we talk for just a minute?" I asked.

She didn't fade away so I took that to be agreement, "Vesta, I have no doubt you were a wonderful mother. You didn't have an easy life; I know that to be the truth. However, it is not a good idea to be talking to Corrie. I know you would do anything to protect your daughter and Corrie's mother will do anything to protect hers. I know you would never harm her in any way but the living don't really understand the innocence of spirits. Can you understand this?"

She stood unmoving for a moment and then nodded her head.

"Please feel free to talk to us. We're here to help you. I know it must be so very difficult for you to trust but you can trust us."

She raised a hand and placed it over her heart then faded away.

"Who are you talking to?" Wally whispered behind me making me jump and my heart skip a beat.

"It's complicated," I said and turned to kiss him. "Good night, I love you."

Chapter Fourteen

After some discussion, Wally and I decided to fly to Washington D.C. Spirit really wanted to stay with Miss Vera. To be a wolf, he sure did like to be pampered. Besides, this was the first road trip Wally and I were able to take since he came home. It would be nice to just think about us for a while.

Miss Vera secured the airline tickets and a rental car. We were catching the red-eye out. In about three and a half hours we would be in the nation's capital. I was looking forward to seeing the hotspot for all things political. I'd seen the pictures on TV, now I would see it as it really was. I don't know about Wally but I slept for a little while. It was amazing to me that I felt so relaxed, unlike the road trip with Aunt Jo when one catastrophe after another kept me on guard.

We landed at Dulles and rented a car. We found a nice hotel and unloaded our luggage. Wally wanted to nap, I wanted to explore. After a hearty breakfast, he went back up to the room and I walked out to the car and headed to the Washington Mall.

I don't know what I expected of Washington D.C. but I know it wasn't this. It's a city of contrasts. Stark, definitive contrasts. Grand government buildings and beside them, slums with windows missing, trash on the ground, and people sitting on the stoop of their apartment buildings. You saw men and women in business suits, carrying briefcases, hurrying down sidewalks. They passed by the homeless hoping to gain a coin or two or even bathing in national monuments. It made me dizzy. I finally found a place to park in a parking garage close to the Air and Space Museum. This place was huge! I walked the Smithsonian mall and wondered if perhaps there was going to be some kind of demonstration. I certainly did not want to get caught up in that and by the look of all the tents set up on the mall, it was going to be a big one.

I veered off and found myself at the Museum of Natural History. I slipped inside and immediately felt the reverence of vast history push against my chest. I approached a desk that had a large sign suspended above it. INFORMATION.

A youngish woman looked up at me and smiled, "How may I help you?"

I should have thought this through. I had no idea what to ask.

I stood rooted to the floor, her smile unwavering, "Umm…this is my first time in D.C."

"It is a fascinating city," she replied.

"Yeah, it really is," I agreed.

"Do you have a question about any of the exhibits? You may find it helpful to rent these headphones. When you push the button on the display, you will hear all about the display. It's really quite interesting," she suggested.

"Oh, yeah, how much to rent them?" I said pulling my wallet out of my backpack.

"They are $24.95 but that's for all day," she replied.

"Oh, how much for just a couple of hours?" I asked.

Still that smile, "$24.95."

"Okay. You know what? I think I'll just wander around for a while," I put my wallet back. "Hey, I noticed on my way in that there are a lot of tents set up out there. Is there some event happening?"

She shook her head, "No. Those are the homeless. They spend their nights on the mall. They will probably be mostly gone in about an hour."

"Homeless?" I said astonished.

She nodded but I could see in her eyes a great wealth of disapproval.

I returned her nod, thanked her, and slowly walked away. The size of this museum was overwhelming. Stairs, darkened hallways, the smell of ancient artifacts, and skeletons of the Woolly Mammoth and a Tyrannosaurus Rex. I wandered down a hallway and found an entire section dedicated to the Native Americans. I dutifully read the placards and studied the pottery, the meaning behind the beaded patterns, weapons, animal furs, and in the more modern display, pictures of tribes. I could feel myself getting sucked into their…wait a minute. I leaned closer to the glass. My breath fogged in front of me. My eyes were glued to one particular picture. A tribe of Sioux. The woman in the back. I felt my eyes were playing tricks on me because I felt I couldn't focus enough to clearly see. I had a strange feeling in my gut. I would have to ask Aunt Jo if she had Sioux ancestry. That woman sure did look like her. I had heard about people having twins, what were they called? I thought as I stared at the picture. Dopplers? No, that wasn't right. Dop…dop…doppelgangers! That was it! I was standing here looking at Aunt Jo's doppelganger! I smiled. I couldn't wait to tell her.

As I exited the display I noticed a clock. Oh my God! I had been in this one museum for over three hours! Wally would be frantic. I hurried out throwing a wave to the woman at the desk. She didn't even look up.

I screeched into the hotel parking lot and took the stairs two at a time to the second floor. I ran down the hall with room numbers flashing by. I found our room and unlocked the door. Wally was in the shower. I could hear him singing My Girl. I plopped in the chair that felt chiseled from granite. He came out with a towel around his waist. If he was surprised to see me, he didn't show it.

"Hey," I greeted him.

"Hey," he said back and leaned over me to kiss the top of my head. He smelled of soap and shampoo. "Have fun?"

"Yeah, I did. I went to the Museum of Natural History," I said.

"That's probably my favorite of all the museums," he said as he pulled clothes from his suitcase. He turned to face me. We just kind of looked at one another for a few seconds and then my trance broke.

"OH! Oh, yeah. Listen, I'm going to go downstairs and get us some coffee," I shot out of my chair.

"You're welcome to stay," he said seductively.

"Oh, yeah, no, I think…you know, you always…I'm going to get coffee," I stuttered as I backed toward the door. I was really starting to worry about our wedding night.

As I was filling our cups with hot coffee, a woman emerged from the kitchen carrying a large pan of scrambled eggs. She smiled at me.

"I'll be bringing out more bacon in just a minute," she said cheerfully.

"Oh, that's okay. I just really needed coffee for now," I replied.

"Where you from?" she asked as the pan clattered into the warming bin.

"Boulder Colorado," I answered. "We're here to visit the Holocaust Museum."

"Oh, I love that museum," she said. "Well, love may not be the right word. It's…it's…sobering."

"How so?" I asked.

The smile slipped a bit, "It's so sad to think just how cruel humans can be to one another. Yet…I find it awe-inspiring to think of the courage and spirit of the Jewish people."

"You sound like you know quite a bit about it," I said by way of a compliment.

"I did my thesis on the Holocaust when I was in college," she explained.

"College?" I regretted the surprise in my tone. A college-educated hotel cook. Was I really that much of a snob?

She laughed, "Yes, I went for business management. I just do this a few days a week for some extra money. The rest of the time, I'm manager for a chain of stores in Baltimore."

"You're very ambitious!" I said in silent repentance for my snobbery.

She laughed, "Ambitious? Got three little ones at home. Now, that's ambitious!"

I really liked this woman.

"Hey! Maybe you'll see the Angel of Sorrows!" she said.

"Who?" I puzzled.

"It's this lady who sits in the museum. Every day. She just sits there staring at a wall-sized photo exhibit. Lordy, I don't know how long she's been going there but she was there every day when I was doing my thesis. It's just something that occurred to me one day. I felt she needed a name instead of 'that woman', so I called her the Angel of Sorrows."

"Did you ever speak to her?" I asked.

"Sure! But between you, me, and the fence post, I think she's a deaf-mute," she said softly.

"Dottie! The bacon's been ready to put out!" a male voice wafted from the kitchen.

She lay a hand on my arm, "I have to go! Please, let me know what you think of the museum, okay?"

"Sure! Thanks!" I said to her retreating back. I was intrigued, to say the least.

"There you are!" I heard Wally call out. "We're going to have to talk about these disappearing acts."

"Is this the kind of nagging I can expect when we're married?" I teased.

He playfully chucked me under the chin. Realizing the coffee was probably cold by now, I lamely handed him the cup, "Sorry." Like a trooper, he drank it but the way his eyebrows came together, I guessed it wasn't as good cold as it was hot. He replaced it with a fresh cup and led me to one of the little café tables.

"So what's on the agenda today?" he asked.

"The Holocaust museum," I said without hesitation.

"That place you went to this morning sounded interesting," he argued.

"After we do what we came here to do," I said firmly.

"Holocaust Museum, here we come!" he said raising his cup.

Chapter Fifteen

We pulled into a parking spot in the garage across the street.

Wally started to get out but I lay my hand on his arm, "Wait. Wait just a second."

He looked at me with concern, "What's going on, Red? You okay?"

I swallowed hard over a lump in my throat. How could I describe the feelings running rampant in my chest, my head, my stomach? I felt…guilty. Guilty? So much suffering and no one did anything, not even me. My brain said of course I didn't do anything! I wasn't even born yet! But my heart said someone should have done something…anything. Was it right for me to go inside that building and just walk through gazing at their suffering? Their pain was on display and still no one will do nothing to stop it. The debt lay heavy upon me.

The building was imposing and intimidating. It looked like a prison to me. Huge, sanded stone blocks with few windows and a stark façade. My stomach was stomping around my gut in heavy boots. I realized I was taking a deep breath with about every other inhale. It was dark and quiet inside. It reminded me of a funeral home where people whispered or kept their thoughts to themselves.

"Welcome," the information clerk greeted us. He was an older gentleman with a balding head and thick glasses. He wore a Yarmulke, a white broadcloth shirt, and a long black coat. A well-trimmed long white beard hung from his chin.

I nodded to him and smiled as I approached him. "Are you the curator?"

He smiled, "No, miss. I am here to answer any questions or to help guide you through the museum."

His voice was gentle and reverent.

Wally leaned in around me, "We would like to talk to the curator. We're looking for something in particular and thought perhaps it may be in a catalog or in a display."

Our guide's smile slipped, "We are not in the habit of disclosing the artifacts of the museum."

I felt we were losing him and our hope of getting information on the wedding quilt. "Oh, no, sir, we aren't wanting to do anything nefarious. We're looking for a particular wedding quilt. We just need to know where we might be able to locate it so we can report back to the family that it is safe."

He hesitated, no doubt wondering if he should fetch the curator or call security. I was holding my breath. I could feel waves of distrust surround me. Generations of distrust. Desperation to hold onto what little they had left.

"Please, if you could just call the curator. If he can't help us, we'll leave but it is very important we see him," I said softly. I didn't know how to reassure him we were the good guys.

He lifted the phone and spoke to someone. He nodded his head, "I understand."

"Dr. Weiss is currently in a meeting and unavailable," he said replacing the phone in its cradle.

"We'll wait," I replied.

"I don't know how long it will be," he said trying to brush me off.

"That's okay, we'll enjoy your...beautiful museum until he can see us. Thank you for checking," I said stubbornly.

We turned away from the desk and slowly walked into the exhibition wing. My chest felt heavy. It was hard to breathe. We looked at the exhibits and we didn't speak. An exhibit of children's shoes hit me particularly hard. Wally was reading every word on the plaques, I just observed and moved more quickly than he. Soon I realized I had left him behind and I wandered into the darker depths. A wall-sized photo of the Auschwitz camp filled the wall with haunted eyes, skeletal frames, a desperate plea for help. Sitting on a bench staring at the photo was a woman. She had very long black hair, her skin looked like fine porcelain, her hands folded demurely on her lap. She wore a long black dress and an embroidered shawl wrapped her shoulders. She appeared rather young, perhaps in her late twenties. The Angel of Sorrows?

I drew a breath and slowly walked to the bench and sat down. I wanted to say something but a tiny voice told me to be still. Just sit with her and be still. I looked at the photo with her. We sat for several minutes. I wanted to approach her but I didn't know how.

"I can hear them," she said so softly I wasn't sure if it was her or my inner voice.

"Pardon?" I asked.

"I can hear them. I come every day to listen to them," she said not taking her eyes from the photo.

Was I supposed to say something? What?

"You hear them too," she said slowly turning her head.

I shook my head, "No, I cannot hear them but I feel them."

Her startling blue eyes bore into me.

"You are one of the chosen ones," she said.

"Chosen? No, I'm here to find something for someone," I said quickly. "May I ask your name? I'm Probably Magic," I held out my hand. She remained immobile.

"I know who you are," she said.

"You do? How...have we met?" I was taken aback by her steady countenance.

"My name is LeLonna. I am an immortal."

Great! I was talking to a crackpot!

LeLonna turned to me with a smile, "I am not a crackpot. I am an immortal."

"I don't know what that means," I was embarrassed that she could read my thoughts.

She didn't answer me. I was quickly learning that the spirit world was not much on explanations and really big on talking in riddles.

"What do they say to you?" I asked changing the subject.

"They do not want to be forgotten," she answered.

"They haven't been forgotten," I assured her. "The Holocaust is being taught in schools and beautiful museums have been created so they are never forgotten."

"That is the lesson. That is history. See the man squatting by the corner of the fence over there? His name is Levy Braun. He was twenty-nine years old when he was shipped to a concentration camp. He was forced to work in the mines for hours with no food, no medical attention, no protection. He was engaged to marry. He died in the ore mines. Do the history books tell you that? Over there is Joseph Meier. He was a hard-working father of four beautiful daughters. Their family was ripped apart and slaughtered. Tell me, did the history books tell you his daughter's names?

Hermann Schmidt was expecting their first child. All of these people were executed for one crime and only one crime...being Jews. That's it. Just being a Jew. They want to know their lives meant something beyond being anonymously recorded in history."

I bowed my head. She was right. We studied the lesson and forgot humanity. Perhaps that was my purpose when spirits showed themselves to me. They wanted to be remembered. They wanted to know that it mattered that they lived and their lives had purpose. It also explained why Vesta was so desperate for the wedding quilt to find its way to Leah.

We sat quietly for a moment. She was listening to the silent cries and I listened to my heart.

"Why can't I hear them?" I whispered.

"You have three golden chains around your heart," she said. "A chain of Distrust. A chain of Suspicion. A chain of Insecurity. You are afraid of being hurt. You are afraid you will not be strong enough. You are afraid you will fail. Once you release those chains, the universe will open for you. You will hear what is whispered in the wind and what is shouted in the storm."

"Why do you come here every day?" I asked her.

She turned to look at me. She looked straight into my eyes, "I have been waiting for you."

She pushed up her sleeve and I had to close my eyes. 952345.

"It's a haunting picture, isn't it?" said a voice behind me.

I turned and looked up into Wally's eyes. I was overwhelmed. I turned back to look beside me but she was gone. LeLonna had delivered her message and now she was gone. I didn't know it then but she had passed the torch. She lay their pain and suffering at my feet and it was up to me to help them find rest.

"I finally convinced the curator to let us look through the catalogs. They are very protective of the artifacts," he said.

I rose and walked to the information desk. "Hi, my name is Probably Magic Sarangoski. I am looking for a wedding quilt that rightfully belongs to Leah Krause. Her parents died during the Holocaust. It was her mother's last wish that her daughter have the quilt passed from generation to generation. I will see the curator now."

"I'm sorry, miss, but…" he began.

"No. I'm sorry that I wasn't clear. You seem to think there are options. There aren't. There is only one. I will see the curator now."

The man blinked several times and I'm not sure but I think I saw fear in his eyes. I stood my ground.

"One minute, miss," he said as he picked up the intercom line.

Two minutes later a very tall, bespectacled man wearing a white Yarmulke with black embroidery appeared.

"May I help you?" he looked from me to Wally.

"Yes," I said with all the bravado I could muster, "I am here to see if you are in possession of a wedding quilt. It is important I return it to the rightful owner. Either you can show me the catalogs and let me look for it or you can take me to the storage area and let me find it myself."

The man hesitated a few seconds.

Wally leaned forward, "If I were you, I'd accommodate this young lady."

"Come with me," he said with a slight bow and led us down a dark corridor and up a short flight of stairs. He opened a door and invited us to come in and sit. I took a deep breath.

"I am Rabbi Weismann. I am the curator of the museum. You can understand our wariness with such a request. We don't let the general public near our…our…historical artifacts."

"I am Probably Magic Sarangoski and I am not the general public. I am here asking about a particular item. I have been asked to deliver a wedding quilt to the rightful owner," I countered.

"As I said, Miss Sarangoski, it really goes against our policy. You see, it is my duty to protect and cherish these items," he said with a smile.

I stood and leaned slightly over the desk, "Then you are no better than the Nazis who stole them in the first place."

The Rabbi's face blanched white as chalk.

"And it is *my* duty to find said quilt and deliver it to the intended party. I am on a quest for Vesta and Jacob Krause. The quilt was intended for their daughter, Leah. Maybe you are like everyone else, perhaps you have it logged under prisoner 556324. That is after all, all Vesta Krause was given after everything else in her life had been destroyed. I'll wait while you look."

Rabbi Weismann's jaw locked. "Come with me," he said tightly.

He led us out into a hallway. I saw LeLonna in the shadows and the very slightest of smiles.

Chapter Sixteen

The warehouse was stacked from floor to ceiling. Boxes, shipping containers, trunks, flat glass panes with documents sealed within. The lighting was terrible. The Rabbi took us down aisles and corridors.

"This will be the section you are interested in. Unless she had the...wedding quilt on her person, it is highly unlikely it is here," he said with a shortness that told me he felt he had no choice but to let me see for myself.

"Thank you," Wally said, "And if we should find it, will there be protocol about releasing it to us?"

The Rabbi said smugly, "First things first. You find it then we'll talk."

I saw a shadow standing silently in a darkened corner.

"There is no way out but the way we came in. I shall have someone at the door constantly until you leave."

With that, he left us to wander among the monstrous collections haphazardly organized.

We started with the five thousands and then walked our way to the fifty-five hundreds. After a three-hour search, we finally found a small box with 556324 stenciled on it. It was too small for a quilt but I wanted to see inside anyway. There was a pitifully small amount. An apron with the Star of David stamped on it. A uniform of dull gray made from a coarse, scratchy material. The log with Vesta's prisoner number on it. Not her name, just her number. I thought about all the things we collect over a lifetime. Photos, souvenirs from vacations, our children's first pictures, brooches passed from mother to daughter, wedding rings, china, all things we accumulate without much thought. Vesta and Jacob had to be in their late sixties, early seventies, and all to show for it was an apron and a uniform, compliments of Adolf Hitler.

"You okay?" Wally asked as he rubbed my shoulders.

"They lived, Wally. They had lives, jobs, children, relatives, happy times, and times of despair. It was all taken away from them. Everything, even their names," I felt like crying.

"I know," he said softly.

The shadow in the corner moved. I could barely make it out.

"Would you mind continuing to look around here?" I asked not taking my eyes off the shadow.

"Sure. We'll keep looking if we have to go through every single box," he smiled.

I walked toward the shadow, it moved across the wall. I followed. It led me deeper into the cavernous dark. My heart was beating against my chest leaving me a little breathless. I had no idea who was leading me away. It could have been Brendore for all I knew but I knew I had to follow.

It stopped and pointed. I saw a door. "What's behind the door?"

The shadow continued to point.

"If you were me, you'd be real skeptical about just going through a door with no knowledge what's on the other side," I reasoned.

The shadow pointed.

"What if it's locked? You expect me to break it down or something?"

The shadow didn't move.

"You need to brush up on your conversational skills," I grumbled.

I looked closely at the door. A door. Pretty innocuous under normal circumstances. I glanced at the shadow. Still there. Still pointing. I hesitantly tested the doorknob. It didn't turn.

"See? It's locked. I am not going to break it down. Maybe I'm not meant to see what's on the other side. You know, not all doors lead to something good. Let me tell you from..."

The lock softly clicked and the door opened just enough for me to know I was, indeed, meant to go through, at whatever the cost.

"Okay! But if something terrible happens to me, that's on you, buddy," I warned.

I took a deep breath and pushed it open. I leaned in to give it a pre-emptive look/see. Pitch black. I couldn't see a thing. The curiosity was kicking in. I stepped through the doorway and felt the wall for a light switch. A dim light burst forth. At first, it seemed like a blinding flash because it was so dark but as my eyes got accustomed, I realized just how dim it was. The light was the least of my focus though. It was a relatively small room. There were boxes on shelves, plastic totes, clear plastic bags, and a bin of nothing but shoes. I looked at the shoes. Worn with holes in them, some held together with rags. Baby shoes, toddler shoes, child shoes. I felt the tears well up. There were plastic bags of striped uniforms. They had been vacuumed packed but I could see a tag on the left side with a number. I walked deeper into the room. I touched the boxes that had no detail written on them beyond a generic label. Dentures, pocketbooks, wedding rings, gloves, I couldn't quit looking. One box caught my eye. I walked over to it and gently removed it from its slot. It simply said, BONES.

I opened it and saw bone fragments, a rib, an entire foot skeleton. My heart was about to beat out of my chest. Why was there a box of bones? Did they use these for a dramatic, grisly display? Then I began to get angry. Why weren't these returned to the families for a proper burial? Why weren't they laid to rest? I replaced the box but I could feel my hands trembling. I continued down the aisle and up the next one. Then I saw it. I knew what it was even before I picked it up. Vacuumed sealed, lost among the stacks of memories was the Wedding Quilt. I pulled the package out. It was horribly yellowed with jagged edges of water stains but there was no mistaking the garland of green with the tiny pink roses. Each panel held a memory from previous generations. I held it tightly against my chest, sank to my knees, and wept.

I don't know how long I stayed there weeping for the indescribable cruelty humans have locked inside. Not only the cruelty but the masterful ability of manipulation. I cried for six million human beings who did not understand just how cruel another human could be until it was explained to them with starvation, beatings, sickness, and a God who chose not to deliver them. I looked at the doorway where the shadow still stood guard. I hated the shadow for making me enter this room of hatred personified. I loved the shadow for leading me to the Wedding Quilt. I eventually ran out of tears. My chest hurt, my eyes felt swollen, and my face felt hot and flushed. The shadow gestured to me that it was time to leave. I rose and walked to the door reluctantly leaving the bones, the shoes, the dentures behind. I flipped the light switch and the room was swallowed in pitch once again. I closed the door and my fingers lingered for a moment.

The shadow had disappeared. I wasn't sure how to get back to Wally. I angrily shouted to apparently nothing, "Thanks for leaving me in the middle of nowhere!"

I wandered until I heard voices. Sound can travel. It can sound close but be far away. It can sound like it's coming from one direction but the origin is in a totally different direction. I just walked. Sooner or later, something was bound to look or sound familiar.

"RED?" I heard Wally call.

"I'm coming!" I yelled back. "Where the hell are you?"

"Just keep coming toward my voice."

"Your voice sounds like it's coming from every direction!"

"Well, just keep walking!"

I kept walking still hugging the quilt to my chest.

Eventually, I heard murmurs.

"Look at the boxes! What are the numbers?"

I looked, "In the two thousands!"

"Okay, you're getting close!" Wally replied.

Down a few more aisles and I could definitely hear voices. I picked up my pace, practically running toward the voices. I saw Wally and Rabbi Weismann standing in the middle of the aisle. As I got closer, I saw the Rabbi's eyes open wide and his mouth pull in tight disapproval.

"You were not supposed to touch anything, just look for the item you seek," he scowled.

"I found it!" I said to Wally totally ignoring the Rabbi.

"Where did you get that?" the Rabbi would not be ignored.

"It was in a room in the back. Off away from everything else!" I said with the excitement of my found treasure.

"What back room?" he asked through narrowed eyes.

"Well, I don't know. How many backrooms are there?" I asked hotly.

"Those rooms are locked," he said stonily.

"No, it wasn't," I argued.

"It was locked," he persisted.

"Okay. But then it was unlocked," I huffed.

"No one is allowed in that room."

"Then you should make sure it stays locked," I said.

"Okay, everyone calm down," Wally said trying to be the voice of reason.

"I'll take that now," the Rabbi said reaching for the quilt.

"Over my dead body! This belongs to Vesta and Jacob's daughter, Leah," I retorted swinging my body away from the Rabbi.

"We'll send it to her," he said. "Let's go upstairs to my office and I'll get her information. I promise I'll see to it she gets it."

I pursed my lips, "Ummm…well, I don't have any information except her name."

I could plainly see his patience was wearing very thin but there was no way I was letting go of this quilt.

"You what?" he growled.

"I only know her parent's name and her first name," I admitted.

Wally stepped between us, "Okay, Rabbi Weismann, Red has been in contact…of sorts…with Mr. and Mrs. Krause.

It is extremely important that the quilt make it to the daughter. Let me tell you, if anyone can track someone down, it's Red. You may be assured that the quilt will not end up on eBay or in some private collection. It will be delivered to Leah, the daughter, as it was intended."

"I think I need to call security. I've had about enough of this foolishness," he said as he turned away.

"Wait!" I said reaching for his arm.

"What?" he snarled.

"In that room. I saw shoes, and personal items, and...and bones," I said thinking fast. "Why haven't those bones been identified and sent to surviving family members so they can lay their loved ones to rest?"

"They had no way to identify them in the forties," he said tightly.

"But they do today!" I pointed out. "If they can identify dinosaur bones millions of years old, surely they can identify bones a mere seventy years old."

"Do you have any idea of the cost of doing that?" he argued.

"As much as letting the public, particularly the Jewish community, finding out you have the very life essence of their ancestors locked in a back room?" I said slyly.

"Young lady, I don't appreciate your thinly veiled threat."

"What if I made sure it was paid for?" I asked.

"Red, what are you doing?" Wally asked from the corner of his mouth.

Rabbi Weismann looked at me long and hard.

"Let me get the quilt to Leah and I swear to you, I will pay to have those bones identified and sent to family," I pleaded.

"Red?" I could hear the panic in Wally's voice.

"Can I have that in writing?" the Rabbi asked.

"Yes! I'll give you all the information," I said quickly.

"Come to my office and we'll continue our conversation," he said. He didn't wait for us to follow, he just turned on his heel and started walking. We hurried to catch up to him. I didn't dare look at Wally but out of the corner of my eye I could see him trying to get my attention.

Suddenly the Rabbi stopped and I ran into him bouncing off his back. He turned slowly.

"What did your friend mean when he said you were in contact…of sorts…with Mr. and Mrs. Krause?"

"It's complicated," I said feeling like I'd been caught in the cookie jar.

"Try me," he said folding his arms across his chest.

"I communicate with the dead," I said simply.

He stared at me for what seemed like several minutes. "I fully intend to drink myself into a stupor when this day is over…*if* it's ever over." He turned and we continued our journey.

I glanced at Wally, he was mouthing the word, *What?* I shrugged.

Chapter Seventeen

After I left information that just stopped short of my bra size, we were on our way. We were escorted to the door which was already locked. The doorman ushered us out and I half-expected to feel a swift kick to my rear. I am positive, though, that had the door not been hydraulic, it would have slammed at our backsides. I didn't care. I had the quilt in my possession. That was all that mattered.

Wally was quiet on the drive back to the hotel. Streetlights flashed by my window and the flashing of turn signals strobed against the night sky.

"Wow, that was some day, huh?" I said to make conversation.

"Uh-huh," he responded, unsatisfactorily if you wanted to know the truth.

"An amazing place. So many emotions..." I said carefully watching his face.

Silence.

"We got the quilt! Yay us! Right?" I said patting the package on my lap.

"I'm just curious..." he began, "do you ever think about what you're saying? Or does it just pop into your head and out your mouth?"

Uh-oh, I was in trouble. I can't pretend I didn't know what he was mad about but I also didn't have an answer to thwart any attack.

"I say what I have to say to get the job done," I replied absolutely defensive.

Wally nodded his head but by the steel cabled cords running up his neck, I could tell nothing could be further from a nod of agreement.

"Soooo...I'm just curious, where are you going to get the funds to pay for DNA testing for who knows how many bones?"

"I'm going to talk to Miss Vera. She said she funds all these missions I go on," I snapped.

Wally swung his head toward me, "Miss Vera? Red, exactly how much do you think it costs to do such an undertaking?"

"I don't know. A couple thousand?" I could feel my underarms start to sweat.

Wally laughed, he RUDELY laughed! "How about you bump that up into the millions?"

I felt like someone just roundhouse-kicked me in the gut. Now, the palms of my hands were sweating, the soles of my feet, I'd bet anything sweat was squirting out of the top of my head! Millions? We were talking money, dollars, moolah, bread.

"I may not have thought this completely through," I was trying really hard to keep my breath steady. I was losing the battle. I smiled at him weakly, "We got the quilt!"

He shook his head, "Holy crap, I'm afraid to go home."

We caught the red-eye out of Dulles Airport. Since no Federal Marshalls yanked us out of line, I figured we were pretty safe. The flight was uneventful and I do mean uneventful. Wally hardly said two words to me.

The drive from the Boulder airport to home was equally quiet. When we arrived Wally went inside without me. When I got our backpacks inside and the quilt in my room, I went into the kitchen where Wally was rummaging through the upper cabinets.

"What on earth are you looking for?" I asked.

"Found it," he said as he removed a bottle of Jack Daniels. He poured a hefty drink and downed it in one gulp.

"I didn't know you drank whiskey. I only ever saw you drink beer," I observed.

He looked at me with bleary eyes, "Girl, if I'm going to be marrying you, I figured I'd better upgrade."

I could see right now this day was going to end with a fight. However, we were engaged, about to say those words, for better or for worse, so I walked over, pecked him on the cheek, and said, "I love you. Thank you for going with me." Then I went to bed.

By the time I rolled out of bed it was nearly noon. I didn't know what kind of shape Wally was in after he visited with Jack but I felt like I was the one who overindulged. Hair frizzed and in my eyes, face swollen, and bones that felt like someone had taken a baseball bat to me, I shuffled into the kitchen.

There sat Wally and a gentleman I'd never met. I stopped short. I slightly swayed. Wally and the man stopped their conversation and looked at me expectantly. I scratched my head.

"Ummm…good morning?" I croaked.

"Well, it's almost noon but okay," Wally said trying not to laugh. I could have slapped him.

I didn't know if I should turn around and go back to my room, or just pretend it's all cool, man, just gettin' some mornin' java, man.

"This is Professor Reed," Wally introduced his still smirking friend.

"Hey," I greeted him.

"This is my lovely bride to be," Wally said behind a smile.

"Cool. Can you excuse me a moment?" and I fled the room.

In my little sanctuary, I tried to clear the sleep fog in my head. I quietly tiptoed into the bathroom and started the shower. I could feel life returning to normal as the hot water poured over me and my muscles relaxed. There. Now, I felt human. I stepped from the shower and grabbed a towel and dried off my body. I reached for my robe and…well…I'd forgotten to bring it in with me. I looked at my dirty pajamas laying on the floor. I just couldn't bring myself to put them back on. I was clean and sweet-smelling. My room wasn't in line with the kitchen so…I could make a mad dash to my room with no one the wiser. I opened the door a crack and breathed a sigh of relief. The coast was clear. I could still hear Wally and the professor talking. I wrapped the towel around me, threw open the door, and tensed my body for the run to safety. BAM! Except it wasn't a run to safety. I ran smack into the professor. I hit him so hard we cracked foreheads and we both landed on the floor! I don't know about him but I was seeing stars! My tailbone certainly didn't appreciate the sudden contact with the hardwood floor.

"Oh my God! I am so sorry!" he shouted as he scrambled to his feet. "Let me help you!"

I held out a hand to stop him, "No! No, no, I'm okay." I shook my head to clear it. My towel had slipped to my waist.

"What the hell are you two doing?" Wally shouted. Then he saw me naked to the waist.

Professor Reed's face was blood red while mine had lost all blood. I grabbed the towel and wrapped it around me as best I could. Wally helped me up.

"I am so sorry. I just...well, I asked if I...oh, my God, I'm so...let me...can I help?" the professor kept apologizing.

"Yes, you can turn around while I put myself together," I snapped.

He looked surprised as he realized he was still facing me with everything my mother's DNA gifted me with. He quickly turned around, "I cannot tell you how sorry I am..."

I ran to my room and slammed the door. I threw myself on the bed and kicked my feet like a two-year-old having a tantrum, complete with thrashing my head and punching the bed with balled-up fists.

After I calmed down, I got dressed but there was no way in hell I was going back out there. There was a soft tap on the door.

"Red? You okay, Sweetie?" came Wally's sweet voice.

"Go away," I snarled.

"Honey, he's gone now," he could be so patronizing.

I barely opened the door, "You sure?"

"Yes, I walked him to the door myself," he assured me.

"Oh, God! I'll never be able to face him again," I whined.

Wally snickered and I gave him a withering glare.

"If it's any consolation, I think he was so got he didn't even notice you were naked," he said trying to make me feel better. He touched my forehead, "You're gonna have quite the goose egg there."

I jerked away from him. Why on earth did people feel this overpowering need to touch an injury? It hurts, dammit, keep your hands off!

"Come on, I'll fix you a cup of tea. We'll start over. Okay?" he cooed. He was really getting on my nerves.

I let him lead me to the kitchen but my eyes darted every which way to make sure no one else was in danger of me plowing into them.

The tea helped and I resented that small fact. I was beginning to get a headache.

"Anywho, the professor was in town to pick up a few things and thought he would stop by. I told him about our trip to D.C. and he was really fascinated," Wally continued as though everything was normal. "I told him about the quilt. He wanted to see it and of course, it's in your room so I said another time."

"Thanks," I grumbled.

Wally was getting his bowl out of the cabinet. He pulled down a box of cereal and shook it to make sure there was enough for his bowl. He stopped and turned around, cocking his head.

"Do you have any ideas on how to find this Leah person?" he asked.

"I guess that's where Corrie comes in," I replied sipping my tea.

"So, you're going to have another go at Rosa?"

"Yeah, I guess so. Maybe I'll invite just her to come here while Corrie's in school," I suggested.

"That's a good idea. Corrie would be royally pissed if she heard her mom flat out say no," he chuckled.

"I miss her. The garden misses her too," I said as I envisioned our garden project overrun by weeds.

"Yeah, the garden misses her," Wally agreed with a snicker.

My encounter with the professor was put on the back burner while I called Rosa to invite her over this afternoon.

"You need to talk to Miss Vera too," he crunched on his Cap'n Crunch.

"Don't remind me," I sighed.

"You have the quilt, now it's time to hold up your end of the bargain," he said as though he was speaking to a six-year-old.

"I know!" I snapped.

Spirit came into the kitchen and laid his head on my lap.

"Hey, buddy, you finally decide to get up?" I smiled.

Spirit had been acting strangely for the past few weeks. He seemed depressed. I made a mental note to call Aaron about just doing a routine physical. It was hard to believe Spirit had been with us for six years! He was such a part of the family; it was hard to remember he had wild roots. I leaned down and kissed his head and ruffled his fur.

Deciding there was no sense in putting off the inevitable, I dialed Rosa's phone number.

"Probably?" she answered the phone.

"Hi, Rosa. How's everything?" I greeted her.

"We're doing good," she answered. I noticed her voice didn't sound so strained. "Corrie is doing well in school. I still can't get her to participate in any extra-curricular activities but then I have to step back and realize she'll find her own way to express herself. What's going on with you?"

"Well, I got the wedding quilt," I blurted out. What happened to easing into the request?

"Really? How? What does it look like?" she asked and actually sounded a little excited.

"It's beautiful! Although, it is quite old so it looks…you know, quite old," I said.

"Miss Vera called me to tell me you and Wally went to…where was it…D.C?"

"Yeah, to the Holocaust Memorial Museum," a picture of the box of bones flashed across my brain. "Now, I need to find the daughter who was meant to receive it. I thought maybe Corrie…"

"Mom? Is that Skunk? Let me talk to her," I heard Corrie in the background.

"Corrie's home?" I asked surprised.

"Yes, Probably, it's Saturday," Rosa laughed. She laughed!

"Oh, yeah. Well, duh, it's Saturday! Kids don't go to school on Saturday…" I stammered.

Rosa laughed again, "You want to talk to Corrie before she rips the phone out of my hand?"

"Oh, before you go, I have a question for you," I said quickly.

"Sure."

"I need help with social media to help find the person the quilt belongs to. Is it okay with you if Corrie helps?" I asked holding my breath.

"I don't see why not," she said and I finally allowed myself to breathe. "Just one condition…"

Uh-oh, conditions can be harbingers of doom.

"Just…well…try to limit her exposure to…you know…things," she said.

"Sure, sure. I think that part is about over anyway. Thanks, Rosa. I appreciate it and I know Vesta's daughter will appreciate it."

"I'll send her around this afternoon. And Probably?"

"Yes?"

"I'm glad you called. I've missed you and I'm so sorry for my behavior," she said with a quietness that I could feel as well as hear.

I smiled, "I've missed you too."

We rang off and I turned to Wally, "We're in business now!"

"Once we talk to Miss Vera," he said not as excited as I was that the world was righting itself.

"Party Pooper," I grumbled.

Chapter Eighteen

Miss Vera looked at me bug-eyed, "You promised what?"

"I got the quilt, Miss Vera," I defended myself lamely.

"Probably, what in Sam Hill were you thinking? We have funds for your missions but…" she spluttered.

"I'm sorry. I just…well, don't you have a 'contact' you can use? You always have a contact somewhere…" I was drowning. Wally was no help. He just sat there like a bump on a log with his arms crossed across his chest. So much for a united front.

Miss Vera looked genuinely pained, "Let me think on this, okay?"

"You mean you might have…" I started hopefully.

"Well, you made a promise, so I'll figure something out. Why didn't you call me?"

"That guy, Rabbi something or other, wasn't real cooperative and Miss Vera, don't you agree those bones should be with their loved ones? How awful to be stuck in a box in a cold, dark room for eternity," I sounded like a pouting Corrie.

"I said I'd figure something out," she snapped.

I felt like I weighed a thousand pounds as we walked back to my house. I looked at Wally and snarled, "YOU were no help! I thought you had my back!"

Wally didn't say anything. He most likely wisely decided against saying anything. It was obvious he was dealing with a ticking time bomb.

I stomped into the house and slammed the door in his face. I went into the kitchen and slammed the teakettle on the stove and rattled the dishes around in the cabinet looking for my favorite cup. I have a feeling I had steam coming from my ears at this point. I felt guilty for making such a promise that I personally had no way of fulfilling, I felt mad at myself for doing whatever it took to get my way, I was embarrassed that I thought I could lay absolutely anything at Miss Vera's feet and she'd take care of it. I had taken advantage of her and she knew it, I knew it, Wally knew it and the whole damned world knew it.

Wally came up behind me and caught my hand as I neared the point of crashing each and every bit of china against the wall. He kissed me on top of my head. I felt the anger drain from me instantly and I slumped against him in exhaustion. Tears of frustration pooled in my eyes and I couldn't see in front of me.

"I'm so sorry," I sniffed.

"Shhh..." he said as rocked me. "We'll figure something out, the three of us."

"Like what?"

"Honey, I don't know just yet but I do know, there's nothing we can't do if we're together. None of us are stupid people, we're just emotional right now. Give us a chance, okay?" he whispered in my ear.

"Where was this support a few minutes ago?" I whined.

"It was where it's always been," he said. He turned me around and smoothed my hair from my face. "Red, think about all the impossible situations we've been in. We've always found a way to work them out, right? We'll figure this one out too. I've been thinking about something,"

"What?" I hiccupped.

"I don't want to jinx it by talking about it right now but I have an idea," he said wiping away my errant tears with his thumb. "Trust me. Trust Miss Vera. Trust us. Can you do that?"

I nodded and at that very moment I felt like I should get a cookie or something to show I was forgiven. Instead, the door burst open and Corrie rocketed right into our hug.

"Hey! Who invited you to a group hug?" Wally teased her.

"I'm special. I don't need no stinkin' invitation!" she laughed.

"One would think you kinda sorta missed us," I smiled as I hugged her back.

"I missed Spirit," she said.

Spirit heard his name and pranced into the kitchen, that big wolf grin on full display. Corrie dropped to her knees and buried her face in his fur as he joyfully slurped her face. I realized slowly but surely; the world was coming back together.

Though it was late afternoon, we made a lunch of spaghetti and meatballs, salad, and buttery garlic bread. Corrie talked non-stop, catching us up on the happenings of a twelve-year-old girl, unlike any other twelve-year-old girl. We laughed and ate good food and eased back into our normal routine of banter. She even helped clean up the kitchen. Wally retrieved our laptop and set it on the table.

"Corrie, I need your help," I said. The love I had for this girl threatened to leak from my heart to my eyes and down my cheek. I had missed her so much over the past few weeks.

"Skunk, I hate to be the one to tell you this but there's no helping you. You are what you are. Embrace it," she said dramatically.

Wally busted out laughing, "Gotcha!"

"Yeah, yeah, yeah, whatever," I snapped but I wasn't mad. I was in heaven. All the pieces were back together and like Wally said, together we could do anything.

I explained to her what we needed and she listened intently.

"I don't know, maybe a picture of the quilt?" I suggested. "Can we do that?"

"If you're wanting to find someone to claim it, then you'll need a way for them to identify themselves," Corrie pointed out. "Otherwise, you'll have crackpots claiming it and the next thing you know, it'll be on eBay for sale. Do you have any social media?"

"Um. No, not really," I confessed.

"Okay, we'll make an account for you," she said as her fingers flew across the keyboard. "Here, stand over by the window."

Not sure what she was up to, I obeyed. "You too, Wallace," she commanded.

Wally raised an eyebrow, "Wallace? Yes, ma'am!"

We stood in front of the window like a happy couple and Corrie snapped a picture with her phone.

"What's that for?" I asked.

"Your profile," she said absently. She studied the picture. "You probably should have brushed your hair, geez."

Unconsciously, I smoothed my hair.

After a couple of hours, she sat back and turned the laptop around for us to see her handiwork. I felt a little uncomfortable as I thought about an entire world gawking at a picture of Wally and me standing at the kitchen counter. I was somewhat surprised that I was so much taller than Wally. We looked…well…for lack of a better word, ordinary. There were pictures of our garden, of Spirit romping in the back forty, a picnic with Corrie, everyday pictures that could have come from any one of a million households across the country. Where were the demons and the spirits? I was stuck on the very ordinary life on display, except our lives were anything but ordinary. People were starting to comment, people I did not know, yet through this one act, they stepped into my life as though I just showed up late to a party.

"Well, what do you think?" Corrie asked proudly.

"Ummm…" I responded.

"What?" she snapped.

I kind of came out of my trance, "No, it's fine."

"Fine?" she repeated.

"Where'd you get all those pictures?" I asked her.

She held up her phone, "Ah, the wonders of technology. You should try it some time."

I shook my head trying to clear it of the numbness of seeing myself in such an innocent rendering. It just didn't feel right. I felt so disconnected from the red-haired Amazon in those pictures. I'm not even sure what I expected but this definitely was not it.

Wally saved me, "How do we go about finding out about the quilt?"

I still couldn't tear my eyes from myself staring at me.

Corrie shook her head at me, "We'll put up a generic post. We don't want to give too much away to keep people from just claiming to be family and then selling it on Craig's List or whatever."

How did this little brat get so smart?

"Is it okay? Can I go ahead and post your request?" she asked impatiently and a little stung that I wasn't singing her praises for a job well done.

All of a sudden, I wasn't so sure this was a good idea. I didn't much care for so many strangers being able to take a peek into my life. I felt vulnerable, exposed, if they saw a picture of Wally and me, what else would they be able to see? What if they...you know...asked questions?

Wally came to stand behind me and put his hands on my shoulders. I could feel his fingers, the bend in his finger joints, the heat where his hands lay. To add insult to injury, I felt tears threaten. I could only nod my head. Corrie went from annoyed to concerned.

"Skunk, we can finish this later. You look a little shell-shocked," she said.

"No. I want...to finish this," I whispered.

Corrie began to type, she called it creating a post.

I am looking for any family of Jacob and Vesta Kraut. Please PM me, it's important.

"You misspelled their last name. It's Krause," I pointed out. She made the correction.

"Also, *its important* should be *it's important*," Wally sounded like an English teacher.

"Geez, guys, this is social media, not a college classroom," she grumbled but she made the correction.

"Now what?" I asked.

"We wait," she said. "It'll either work or it won't. I'd better get home though. Give it a few days and we'll see what happens."

After Corrie left for home, I felt disoriented. I kept looking at the laptop on the table as though it had turned into a cobra ready to strike. I kept my distance. I cooked a simple dinner for Wally and me, in the kitchen that millions of strangers now knew what it looked like. They knew the color of the walls. They knew I had wolf canisters sitting on the counter. They knew I had red, frizzy hair. They knew I was taller than Wally. They knew I had a garden. The list went on and on and I felt more and more exposed. Even if I had Corrie take the page down, millions already saw what could not be unseen.

"You're awfully quiet, Red," Wally said.

I looked up at him across the kitchen table. Funny but what was going on inside my head was anything but quiet. "I am?"

"Honey? You wanna talk about it?" He came to sit beside me and held my hand.

I shook my head. It wasn't that I didn't want to talk about it, I just didn't know *how* to talk about it. He kissed me on the cheek.

"Let's get some sleep. By morning, you'll feel differently," he said.

He helped me clean the kitchen and then went to brush his teeth and get ready for bed. When it was my turn, I went in to brush my teeth and somehow ended up in the shower. I let the water flow over me. There weren't any pictures of the bathroom so that was my refuge. I didn't feel prying eyes in there. I kept thinking about that picture of Wally and me. I just wasn't sure how I felt about it…what it represented. The tall, skinny, frizzy-haired little girl who would let no one in her life was now part of a couple. When had that door in my heart opened? I stepped out of the shower and stood peering into the mirror. *Who are you?* I whispered. I dressed in my customary boxer shorts and t-shirt and softly padded to the kitchen. I looked over both shoulders and slowly opened the laptop.

"*Why aren't you in bed?*" someone typed. I jumped as though they were standing behind me.

"*None of your beeswax. Who are you?*" I typed back.

"*Go to bed, Skunk. You're cranky when you're up past your bedtime.*"

"*Corrie? Really? I'm up past MY bedtime?*"

LOLOLOLOL

What in the world did that mean?

"*I wanted to see if anyone answered our post,*" I lied.

"*Give it a couple of days to circulate.*"

"*Oh, okay,*" I answered.

"*Hey, Skunk?*"

"*Yeah?*"

"*You make a rotten liar.*"

"*Go to bed, Corrie, and by the way, who is Sandy?*"

"*That's my online name. Mom says I'm too young to have a page so this way she doesn't have to know.*"

"*That's not right, Corrie. You shouldn't go behind your mother's back.*"

"*How else am I supposed to talk with my boyfriend?*"

"*Your boyfriend? Who's your boyfriend?*"

"*A forty-two-year-old businessman named Armand.*"

"*For real?*"

"*LOLOLOLOL!*"

"You're such a brat! Go to bed!"
"Nite, Skunk."
"Nite, problem child."

I closed the laptop and realized I was smiling. I didn't feel so violated now. This small bit of technology kept me connected to Corrie. She was like a lifeline in cyberspace. I got a drink of water and went to bed. I resisted the urge to peek to see if Corrie did, indeed, go to bed.

Chapter Nineteen

I woke early and went into the kitchen to put the tea kettle on and get pancakes out of the freezer for our breakfast. As I busied myself, every time I walked past the laptop, I looked at it. I vowed to wait until after breakfast to check it. I put the pancakes in the microwave and removed fresh blueberries from the fridge. Maybe just a tiny peek. No! Corrie said to give it a few days. Besides, what did I care about stupid social media? Did Corrie check her bogus account first thing when she woke up? I think the answer to that is a resounding 'no'. She was one of the coolest kids I'd ever known. I felt like one of those introverted weirdos who was befriended by one of the popular kids.

"Good morning!" Wally said as he shuffled into the kitchen. "You're awfully ambitious first thing in the morning. Okay, where's Red and what have you done with her?"

"You aren't funny in the mornings, Wally, don't give up your day job," I snarled.

"Love you too, Beautiful," he laughed.

Without any thought or hesitation, he pulled the laptop over to him and opened it up. Just like that! Just opened it up like it was no big deal!

He began to chuckle, then laughed out loud.

"What's so funny?" I asked moving behind so I could see too.

"This is hilarious," he was laughing hard now.

As I sat his plate in front of him, he pulled me down on his lap. "Take a look."

Sure enough, below the post were lots of comments.

"marie sanders: *I knew some Krauts when I was growing up in KY*"

"benny: *Man, look at that broad. I'd tap that*"

"AlicenChuck: *That is one weird looking couple. I wouldn't trust them.*"

"benny: *gotta get me some of dat*"

"Samantha: *Benny, you're an idiot You need to go play with your inflatable doll*"

"benny: *Samantha, jealous?*"

"Craig L: *They look like hippie Democrats*"

Wally was laughing like a loon. I felt pretty insulted. These people didn't even know us! How could they say such hateful things? I slammed the laptop closed.

"This isn't going to work!" I said through clenched teeth.

"Whoa! Hey, Red, calm down," he said. You would have thought he'd learned by now you do not tell a woman to calm down, especially me. He held up his hands, "What I mean, is that these people know nothing about us. They can say things they wouldn't necessarily say in person because we know nothing about them either."

He did have a point there. "I still don't like them saying stupid crap. What exactly do Democrats look like anyway?"

"Yeah, that was my favorite," Wally snorted.

"Shut up," I hissed.

Corrie came bounding into the kitchen and straight to the refrigerator. As she stuck her head inside searching for whatever, she said over her shoulder, "Did you see it?"

Wally quit laughing and we looked at her foraging in our fridge.

"See what?" we asked together.

"You got a response!" she said happily.

"You mean the guy who wants to have sex with me and the one who said we looked like Democrats?" and the anger bubbled up again.

"No! Closer down to the end. Here, I'll show you," she said as she gently elbowed Wally out of the way.

"Adrian B: *My grandmother's maiden name was Krause but her parents were killed in the Holocaust.*"

I stared at the comment. "What do we do now?"

"We ask her to PM us," Corrie suggested.

"What's PM?" I asked.

"Private message. Geez, Skunk, have you lived your life under a rock?" she said with a sigh of exasperation.

She did a series of clicking and a small box popped up. "What do you want to say to her?"

Nothing like being put on the spot. I couldn't get two words together in an intelligent thought.

Wally stepped in to save me, "Ask her what her grandparents name was."

"Well, you already said in the post you were looking for relatives of Jacob and Vesta Krause," she reminded him.

"Oh, yeah," he was clearly disappointed he hadn't provided any help at all.

"Ask her if she knows what town in what country they were from," now my brain was kicking in.

She typed the question.

"She might not be there right now," I said as I waited for the response.

"Yeah, she's online. See that little green dot? That means she's online," Corrie said pointing to the green dot next to Adrian's name. "She's checking us out."

"How?" I asked and then a reply came through.

"*I need to know what this is about. I'm uncomfortable answering personal questions from strangers. How do you know my grandparents and why are you looking for our family?*"

"Here, move over, Corrie," Wally said as he elbowed Corrie out of the way.

"*We recently came into possession of something from your great grandmother, Vesta. We want to make sure it gets to her family,*" he typed.

"*Like what?*" she asked.

"*An item that is very personal and unique to your family,*" he said vaguely.

There was silence for a moment or two. "*The wedding quilt?*"

'Bingo!" Wally shouted with joy. "We have our family!"

I lay my hand on Wally's arm, "Not so fast. We know nothing about her. I want to talk to her."

"We are talking to her, Red," Wally stated the obvious.

"No, I mean really talk to her. Give her my phone number," I instructed.

"Red-"

"Just do it. If she's a fraud, I'll be able to tell if I hear her voice," I explained.

"Okay…I'm still not sure that's a good idea," he argued.

"I can always change my number," I pointed out.

"Or you can simply block her number," Corrie chimed in. I gave her one of my looks but now wasn't the time to ask for explanations.

"Okay," Wally said as he began to type.

"*Adrian, we have gone through a lot to get this item...the wedding quilt. We're determined it gets to the correct family. Here is our phone number. Would you be willing to call so we can discuss it?*"

"*Are you asking for money?*"

"*No. No money. We just feel it's that important.*"

We waited for about ten minutes. I could imagine her trying to decide if this was a scheme or not. Finally, the phone rang.

I answered, "Hello? Adrian?"

A soft-spoken woman said, "Yes. And who am I talking to?"

"Yes, my name is Probably Magic Sarangoski. That's my real name, I swear, if we meet I'll show you my driver's license. I need to ask you a few questions. Do you mind?"

"Your name is really Probably Magic?" she asked.

"It really is Probably Magic," I smiled. "It's a long story that I'll share at another time. Deal?"

"Okay," but she still sounded skeptical.

"What is your mother's name?" I asked.

Silence.

"Fair enough," I said after I allowed her to be suspicious still. "I'm going to give you three names. You tell me which one is right. Esther, Leah, Rebecca."

"Leah is my *grandmother's* name," she said and it sounded like she may have just given an audible sigh of relief.

"Excellent. Now, can you tell me the location your grandmother was born? France, Germany, Poland?"

"Poland! A little town called Klamry," she now sounded excited.

"Hi, Adrian! I've been looking for you!" the excitement was contagious. "Just one more question, okay? Can you describe the wedding quilt?"

"Well, I've never seen it but Mom told me about it. She passed away two years ago but my grandmother spoke of it often. Many, many times. It was white with pink roses, the Star of David, a green leafy garland border, and the names of each of my grandmothers as they passed it down," she described the quilt to a tee.

"Adrian, is your grandmother still living?" I asked.

"Technically she is," she said sadly. "She has dementia. I tried to care for her as long as I could but I finally had no choice but to put her in assisted living."

I felt a gut punch, "I'm so sorry."

"I think, though, she would be very happy to finally have her quilt. She may not remember me or what she had for breakfast but she has some very clear memories of her childhood," she said. "Will you be sending the quilt?"

I hadn't even thought about how we would get the quilt to her! I had been so focused on just finding her, I hadn't really given a thought about what came afterward. Something in my gut told me that I had to personally hand over the quilt.

"It's far too important for me to trust anyone. I'm afraid it will need to go from my hands to your grandmother." Was this going to be the deal-breaker?

"I understand," Adrian said.

It was my turn to give that sigh of relief.

"Where are you?" I asked.

"We live in Florida," she said.

"Okay, we will deliver it in person," I decided. I dare not look at Wally. I was off doing that anything for the mission thing I always did.

She gave me her address and made plans for the delivery. At the end of our conversation, she gave me her phone number. "And, Probably?"

"Yes?"

She hesitated and when she spoke there was a trembling in her voice, "Thank you. God bless you."

"Sure. I'll just be glad to get it where it truly belongs. Thank you for talking with me," I said barely above a whisper.

We hung up and danged if I didn't break down in tears. Corrie on one side, Wally on the other, enveloped me with their love.

Chapter Twenty

We took Corrie home as it was starting to get dark, mostly because I felt uncomfortable having her ride her bike during the evening hours. When we pulled into the little driveway, she burst out of the car and ran to the front door barely turning the knob before bolting inside yelling for her mom. By the time we stepped onto the porch, Rosa was laughing at her excited daughter.

"Slow down! I can't understand a single word you're saying!" Rosa laughed.

Corrie took a deep breath, "Mama, we found her! We found the lady that the quilt belongs to!"

Rosa looked up at me. I smiled and nodded, "We did! And we couldn't have done it without Corrie's help!"

"Oh, that's wonderful!" Rosa exclaimed. "Please come in and tell me all about it!"

"Mama, they're going to Florida to give it to her in person. Can I go? Please, Mama, can I go with them?" Corrie was talking loud and quick, the excitement visibly making her bounce up and down.

Rosa turned Corrie's shoulder and guided her into the house. Once we were settled in the living room, Rosa smiled, "I want to hear all about it!"

So, we related what we discovered and ended with, yes, we were going to Florida to deliver the quilt.

"See, Mama? I need to go! Can I, please, please, please?" Corrie begged.

"Honey, Florida is a long way away. Probably and Wally are not going on vacation, they're going for a specific reason. I'm afraid you would be in the way and besides, you've never been away from home that long," Rosa tried to reason with her bouncing daughter.

"It's okay with us if she goes," Wally said. I looked at him surprised. Sure, I did things without checking with anyone else, but Wally?

"Oh, I don't know, she has school, you know," Rosa said uncertainly.

"Mama, just think, I'll be learning about history! A real live person that lived the history we study in class!"

I felt obliged to clarify, "Well, no, you won't. Miss Adrian is merely a granddaughter; she wasn't actually there during the Holocaust and neither was her mother."

Corrie turned around and gave me one of those death ray looks she was so good at, "Skunk, really? You're not helping? Wally said it was okay. And, Mama, I promise to be on my best behavior. I won't be any trouble; they won't even know I'm there."

Helpless, I shrugged.

"What do you think, Probably? I'd feel better if she stayed here," Rosa looked to me for reinforcements. A good friend would acquiesce to a mother's concerns but...

"We'd never let her out of our sight," I offered. "I think she would enjoy helping us. After all, she's kinda been there since the beginning."

Corrie looked at her mother grabbing her hands, "See? Please?"

"How long would you be gone?" Rosa asked me but she was looking straight into her daughter's huge, hopeful blue eyes. It would take someone stronger than me to turn down anything those blue eyes wanted.

"Oh, just long enough to drive there, turn over the quilt, and drive back. Should be less than a week," Wally chimed in. I swear, sometimes I think he was as much of a kid as Corrie.

"I don't know…" she hedged.

"When was the last time you had an adventure, Rosa?" I asked.

"Where are you going with this?" she said suspiciously.

"Come with us!" I stunned myself with my brilliance.

"Come with you?" she repeated.

"Sure! Corrie will learn something of history, you'll have a break, we'll deliver the quilt. It's a win-win proposal, if you ask me," I pointed out.

"Oh, my goodness! I haven't been to Florida in years!"

"Come with us, Momma!" Corrie grabbed her mother's hand and was swinging it back and forth. "It'll be fun!"

Rosa's mouth went into a hard straight line. The wheels were turning and if you listened closely enough, you could hear the gears click into place.

"You know what? Okay. Okay, Corrie and I will go with you. Okay."

Corrie screamed in excitement. My ears are still ringing. So, it was settled, the four of us would travel to Florida, deliver the quilt and come straight home.

"Spirit has to go too!" Corrie squealed.

So, it was settled, the five of us would travel to Florida, deliver the quilt and come straight home. You know about the best-laid plans, right?

On Friday morning, we were all standing by the back hatch of the Chevy Tahoe.

"I didn't realize four people needed so much luggage," I whispered.

Wally scratched his head.

"There's no room for Spirit," Rosa observed.

"Oh, yes there is!" Corrie huffed. She started taking suitcases out of the back cargo area.

"Hey!" Rosa caught her arm to stop her.

Wally looked in mocked concentration, "Sorry, Half-Pint but we're gonna have to tie you to the hood."

"Uh-Uh. We'll strap you to the roof!" she exclaimed.

They started playfully swatting at each other.

"Children, play nice," I said sternly. I looked at the back hatch filled with suitcases, bags, coolers, and odds and ends and sighed. "I don't see how we can put him in there. Besides, Miss Vera would miss him something terrible."

Corrie looked up at me with anger in her eyes, "We'll all get rid of two pieces of luggage. That should give us enough room."

"Honey," I tried to reason, "He weighs two-hundred-eighty pounds! He takes a lot of room!"

"Then we all get rid of three pieces of luggage. He has to go!" she insisted

Wally and I looked at each other. We had traveled and hiked enough we could fit a week's worth of supplies in one backpack each. All these suitcases, duffle bags, and bags were Rosa and Corrie's. I didn't want Rosa to feel like she was a bother so I held my tongue.

Corrie pulled out an overnight bag, "What's in this one?"

"Makeup," Rosa said softly. Corrie threw it into the yard, "You're beautiful without makeup."

"What about this one?" she asked accusingly.

"Not sure what I'll need so I packed casual and dressy," her mother said defensively.

"It's hot. You need shorts and t-shirts," Corrie said as she sat it on the ground.

"Young lady, I think you're done," Rosa warned.

"Nope. Not until we have Spirit his own space," she said totally ignoring her mother.

Rosa looked at me helplessly for reinforcements.

"How about this? Let's take the luggage in and just see what we can do without," Wally suggested.

We grabbed all we could hold and marched back into the house. We dumped the luggage on the living room floor and began to sort through it.

I held up a rather large duffel bag. "Corrie? Why do you need a bag of books?"

"So, I can learn more about the Holocaust," she said as though I was an ignoramus.

"I think you're going to learn plenty," I said and set the bag aside.

By the time we finished, we were down to four pieces of luggage. We carried them out to the car and slid them into the cargo hold. Spirit had plenty of room, much to his delight. Rosa was pretty quiet. No doubt thinking she was now totally unprepared for Florida.

Miss Vera came out to wish us well.

"Oh, you all are going to have so much fun!" she clapped her hands as her face beamed.

"Why don't you come with us?" Corrie was now bouncing in excitement forgetting all about leaving her books, four pairs of tennis shoes, laptop, and X-Box behind.

Miss Vera wrapped Corrie in her arms and kissed her on her head, "You are so precious, Corrie. I could just squeeze the puddin' right out of you!"

Corrie laughed and hugged her back, "Why not?"

"Oh, honey, I have things to do here. I have to make sure your rutabagas grow strong, I have to weed the flowerbeds while you're gone, and Probably gave me kind of a big project to do," she looked over her glasses at me. I think I was supposed to feel chastised.

I cleared my throat, "Yeah, well, we'd better hit the road. We're burning daylight."

"Just a minute!" Miss Vera snapped her fingers and hurried back into the house. She came out carrying two plastic containers and a canister. "Just a little something for the road and the canister is for Spirit."

I wasn't sure where I was going to stash them but I would rather have nails poked into my eyes than disappoint Miss Vera, besides, I felt it wise to stay on her good side. I put them on my side of the floorboard.

She went around hugging everyone and we began the ritual of getting everyone situated. Spirit was dancing around and going in circles anxious to find his place.

"Shotgun!" Corrie called.

"Yeah, I don't see that happening," I growled. I must have been out of my mind. What started out as a nice peaceful drive with the love of my life, was now a noisy, disorganized, crazy chaos. *Play nice*, I reminded myself. "Anyone need to use the bathroom before we hit the road?"

Everyone shook their head and started fussing about who was going to sit where.

"Last call for the bathroom," I announced.

"Can we just GO?" Corrie groused.

After what seemed like hours and hours, everyone was finally settled in. Spirit wanted to look over the backseat, Rosa sat in the passenger backseat with Corrie on the driver's side. I sat shotgun and Wally would be the first driver. I breathed a sigh of relief as I closed my door. I was already exhausted. The sun had risen above the horizon with light, wispy clouds tinged with peach and turquoise. Wally started the car, checked his mirrors, made sure everyone was belted in and put the car in gear.

"Skunk?" came a voice from the backseat.

"What, Corrie?" I asked irritably.

"I have to pee," she said softly.

Chapter Twenty-One

We were finally on the road. We sang with the radio, we looked at the scenery, we played the license plate game, we just generally had a good time.

"Mom! Look at the horses! Mom! Look at that old tractor! Mom! What's Florida like? Will we see any alligators? Does Florida have McDonalds? Will we get to see the ocean?"

By the time we hit Missouri, it was more like, "I'm hungry. I'm bored. How much longer? Are we ever going to stop and get something to eat? When are we going to stop at a hotel?"

I have to tell you; I was about ready to jump out of the car. Wally just drove on, never asking if I could drive or saying anything about stopping anywhere. We did though. Around ten o'clock that night, we pulled into a neat, clean hotel chain. No one was saying anything or at least it seemed like it. It might have been because Corrie was asleep against her mother and the car was, at last quiet. Poor Spirit kept shifting his position as he did his own protest of being cooped up in the car for hours on end. I wonder if he still thought it was a good idea to be cooped up in the car with four crazy people.

Wally got two rooms and drove to the back of the hotel. We were on the ground floor, thank goodness. Rosa woke Corrie and guided her to the room like she was a zombie. We were all tired and getting on each other's nerves. I questioned whether this trip was a good idea or not. The mission still loomed in front of us and we still had miles to go. Maybe things would be better in the morning after everyone had a good night's sleep.

Wally had gotten a room with two queen-sized beds. After stretching his legs and eating some dinner, Spirit went to one of the beds and stretched out. Wally looked at the large wolf taking up the bed and sighed heavily.

"You can sleep with me, if you want," I offered.

Wally just nodded, removed his shoes, and lay down. He was asleep in seconds. I, on the other hand, needed a shower so I showered, brushed my teeth, and turned off the lights. I slid into bed, which made Wally snort and flop to the edge. I was tired. I had so much on my mind. I doubted I would get much sleep. My mind was too active, too jumbled up, too aware that the man I loved was snoring loudly right beside me. I lay waiting for daylight, knowing I was going to be exhausted in the morning.

Colors filled the room. The sun streaming through the stained-glass windows, threw yellows, blues, and reds across the walls and carpet. I was standing in this room with my stomach churning and my hands shaking. I sneaked a peek at the mirror and once again, I was simply dumbfounded by the beautiful woman in the mirror. I couldn't seem to connect the beautiful woman to the plain-Jane of my everyday life. My hair was in a loose updo with tiny seed pearls woven through the cascade of curls bunched at the top of my head. My dress was filmy and lacy and white. The neckline exposing my cleavage and accentuating my tiny waist. It fell to the floor into a three-foot train. The veil was trimmed in lace and seed pearls, secured by an emerald tiara. The long sleeves were single-layer lace giving the illusion that the dainty lace was tattooed upon my skin.

"It's time. Are you ready?" Miss Vera stuck her head into the room.

I couldn't speak. I nodded my head. We walked down a long hall and as we walked, my friends from The Third Realm, the tiny seahorse fairies, secured themselves in the lace and veil. My dress was iridescent with the lights of a hundred little fairies. My heart raced. As I reached the sanctuary, my father smiled at me and held out his crooked arm. I leaned over kissing him on the cheek and put my arm through his. We began the Wedding March down the long aisle to the priest standing at the altar. Rosa and Corrie looked lovely in their sage dresses and pink and lavender bouquets. They smiled as they watched us. Corrie stood in line with her mother and stepped forward as we arrived at the altar. Dad kissed me on the cheek saying, "I love you, baby girl," and I handed my bouquet to Corrie.

Wally looked at me and mouthed, "I love you." I smiled and returned the endearment. I realized I was so happy, my eyes started leaking. This made my nose run, and I tried to sniff without sounding like a rooting hog. I loved this man so much. I couldn't believe I was about to pledge my life and love to another person with the vow it would be forever. What would life hold for us? I smiled at him and the returned smile made my heart melt.

The priest turned and my heart slammed against my ribcage. He laughed and gave me a deathly glare. I stood quaking, looking into Brendore's cruel eyes.

"You don't really think I would allow this, do you?" he growled.

"No! Get the hell out of here!" I gasped with the small amount of air in my lungs.

He laughed and I heard the evil cackle of the crow. He raised his arms. The beautiful sun and prisms disappeared. "How much do you love him, Red Probably Magic? What would you sacrifice for him?"

I just kept shaking my head no. No. The doors in the back flew open slamming into the wall on either side. My head jerked toward the sound and I saw the Manoucks fly down the aisle. They started attacking *everyone. I stood screaming. One went for Miss Vera's throat, Aunt Jo started to raise her arms to summon the protective blue aura but she was knocked to the ground. Blood splattered the walls, Mother was screaming, my Father trying to fend for both of them. Blood covered my gown and hung in droplets from my veil. I lunged toward them but Brendore caught me and pinned my arms behind me. He was forcing me to watch the slaughter.*

"*Only you can save them,*" *he howled,* "*What will you give me to stop the attack?*"

I began sobbing within the screams. I screamed and screamed. Brendore laughed and laughed. Two Manoucks began to stalk Wally. I tried to wrest free of Brendore's strength but he only held me tighter.

"*Offer me your first child,*" *he demanded.* "*Your child for your beloved's life.*"

"*No!*" *I screamed.* "*I will kill you!*"

He laughed, "*You can never kill me, Red Probably Magic. We are forever entwined in each other's lives. Submit to me!*"

Exhausted and defeated, I shook my head as the carnage spread before me. I could only close my eyes, "*No, no, no...please, stop. Please, no.*"

"Red, do something!" Wally pleaded. "Do something now!"

The Manouks lunged for him, I let out a primal scream.

"Red!"

"Red!"

"Red!"

I began to swim back into consciousness. I was cold and someone was holding me tight. I fought against them.

"Red, baby! It's okay, I'm here," I heard Wally's voice bubble through the haze. "It's okay. You're safe."

I opened my eyes. Wally was holding me, rocking gently back and forth. "You're safe, shhh...it's okay, sweetheart. I'm here. I will always keep you safe. It's only a bad dream."

Slowly I became aware of the hotel air conditioner softly blowing air, the sliver of light filtering through the drapes, the warmth of the arms holding me. All at once I bolted for the bathroom and vomited.

Shaking and sweating, I sat on the cool floor and tried to get my bearings. I just kept seeing the attack whether my eyes were open or closed. Wally tapped on the door and slowly came into the small room. He sat beside me, holding me. He didn't ask me to relate the dream and I don't think I would have if he had.

Someone knocked on the door.

"You okay? I'm just going to see who's at the door. Okay? You'll be okay?" he asked. I noticed his voice was shaking and his face was extremely pale.

I nodded and I turned and vomited again.

I heard Rosa's voice and just a few seconds later, Wally returned to his seat on the bathroom floor. Spirit was pacing from one end of the room to the other. Back and forth. Back and forth. I could hear him panting.

I looked at Wally and burst into tears. I have never felt so terrified, so helpless, so vulnerable, so weak, as I did that night on the bathroom floor in Arkansas.

Wally led me back to bed and lay with me, holding me. I turned to him, "Kiss me, Wally. Please, kiss me so I know I'm alive. So I know you're alive. So I know we are safe."

Wally leaned in and kissed me. I hungered for more. I hungered to feel something other than the terror that would not leave my mind. I lost my virginity that night. The thing is, it wasn't sexual arousal that caused us to join, it was the coldness that permeated my bones. It was seeking warmth and validation. There really wasn't anything sexual about it but it was pure, untainted love with the hope it would drive out the darkness in my mind.

Chapter Twenty-Two

The next morning we had a healthy serving of uncomfortable silence with our grits and hotcakes. Corrie's eyes darted from one face to another searching for a clue as to why everyone seemed so subdued. I wanted to smile and assure her everything was okay but the words got stuck in my throat. I didn't have an appetite. Food wasn't what I needed. I needed answers.

Had I unwittingly pledged our first child to Brendore? How could I marry Wally knowing that our love child would be taken from us and raised by a demon? Or...how could I sacrifice Wally to save our child and raise it by myself? How could we have a life together with this horror between us? I guessed there would be no stopping Brendore from taking anything he wanted from me. No, I wasn't guessing. I knew in truth he would take whatever he wanted. The more pain it caused me, the better he would like it. How could I keep those I loved safe?

"Babe, you need to eat something," Wally said softly.

I shook my head.

After what seemed like hours, we finally got ready to leave. Wally paid the ticket and followed us out to the car. Without offering to let someone else drive, he got in and started the car. I felt I was made of solid concrete. I felt heavy and detached. Corrie leaned over the seat and hugged my neck. I felt tears fill my eyes. I patted her arms encircling my neck.

"It's okay, sweetie. I just had a horrible nightmare last night. I guess I'm still kind of bugged by it," I said flatly.

"Sometimes I have really bad dreams too," she commiserated.

"Then you know how they can bug ya," I said.

"Yeah, I do. But know what? When I have them now, I always try to imagine myself changing the end. Usually, once I wake up, but I'll replay it in my head and I make a different ending," she said.

I nodded and patted her arms again. She sat back in her seat and I heard the click of the seatbelt. I didn't want to be comforted. I'm not even sure I could be. I just couldn't shake the terror, the helplessness, the feeling that I was a failure.

We drove for several hours with nothing but the radio breaking the silence. We passed through Mississippi and into Alabama. I dozed off and on. My head felt like it weighed a hundred pounds. My body ached. Wally put his hand on my leg and gave it a gentle squeeze. I wondered why he never asked me about the dream and then I was glad he hadn't. I could not share it. It was mine to bear alone. Wally got off on an exit for a small town and we looked for a decent place for lunch.

Back on the road, I once again retreated into my own little world. Corrie was talking non-stop and Rosa was trying to read. Wally was teasing Corrie but I couldn't comprehend nor join in their games. We started to see signs for Memphis, TN. Rosa started talking about Graceland and how she was a huge fan of Elvis Presley, the King of Rock and Roll. I can't say I know that much about him. When I suggested that perhaps we could make a pit stop at Graceland to stretch our legs and take a break from the long drive, it was met with cheers and excitement. I should have kept my mouth shut. We really couldn't spare the extra three hours that took us from our route but it was nice to see everyone so happy to be doing something other than watching the mile markers fly by.

Graceland is the mansion Elvis spent the majority of his life. It's a sprawling estate with tall white columns and a brick exterior. Gardens are meticulously groomed and even though the manor is starting to show some wear, it was still impressive. I had a strange feeling as we pulled into the guest parking lot. Corrie, Rosa, and Wally were excited but I was just glad I could actually walk some of the soreness out of my legs. Could we afford time-wise this little detour? Not really but it was nice to see some excitement and maybe get my head out of the horrible dream.

We bought our tickets and entered the foyer showing the living room. Perfectly preserved I could actually feel that this was the hub of Elvis's personal life. It had a 'living' feel to it. We continued with our tour.

"They must have a café or something," I said. "I could use a snack. What about you guys?"

They looked at me confused. "Don't you smell something baking? I bet they just have things like muffins or rolls."

Rosa and Wally looked at each other. Wally shook his head. I was confused. I definitely smelled something *cinnamony* baking.

"To my knowledge, they don't serve food here," Rosa said chewing her lip.

"Don't you smell it?" I asked.

An Elvis impersonator, I assumed, walked down the hallway turning into a room.

"Well, I'm not crazy. I'll ask that guy who works here," I said as I turned on my heel and pursued the impersonator. There was no one there. I looked around the room for doors that may lead outside. The only doorway was the one I was standing in. My scalp prickled.

"Mr. Presley?" I whispered. "It's okay, I can see dead people. It doesn't scare me so if you want to show yourself, it's okay. You can trust me."

Now, this could go two ways: either people would think I was a nutcase or Elvis really would answer me.

I looked around the room. Bright green shag carpet and carved pillars and furniture filled the room. It kinda felt like being inside a tree, like a gnome's house or something. I saw movement in the shadows. Elvis stepped forward and gave me a crooked smile.

"Hi, my name is Probably Magic," I introduced myself. He looked surprised.

"THE Red Probably Magic?" he asked.

I giggled. You'd think I'd be used to that moniker by now. "In the flesh!" I quipped. "Hey, I'm ashamed to say I really don't know much about you. Apparently, you were kind of a big deal."

His smile grew and I saw a glimmer of those dimples that drove women wild.

"Anyway, the lady I'm with is a huge fan. I'm not going to ask you to show yourself to her or anything, just wanted to let you know you had a big…you know…fan. I do have a question though. Why am I smelling something baking? Is there a café in here somewhere?"

He shook his head, "My mother was a baker. She was always whipping up something in that kitchen."

"Oh," I said and because I was kind of hungry, I felt let down.

He took my program from me and went to the desk and retrieved a pen. "What's your friend's name?"

"Rosa," I said still thinking about muffins and cookies.

He handed my program back and I looked down. *To Rosa, Never pass up the chance to dance. Elvis Presley*

"Oh! Thank…" but he was gone. Now, how was I going to explain this to Rosa? I found our little group and tucked the autographed program in my jean's back pocket.

Back on the road, Corrie looked at the **souvenirs** Rosa bought in the gift shop. Rosa was explaining all about the King of Rock and Roll. She told Corrie about the one concert of his she went to. She said danged if she wasn't screaming and crying and dreaming of being the Fool He Rushed to. Corrie didn't really seem all that interested but for the sake of her mom she was trying.

"Oh, I got this for you," I said passing the signed program back to her.

She took it and looked at it closely, "Where did you get this?"

"Oh, I think Elvis…I mean…the Elvis impersonator…you know, they do stuff like that all the time," I tried to brush it off.

"What Elvis impersonator? I didn't see any Elvis impersonator," she quizzed me.

"Oh, well, you know, they have guys dressed up…"

"I *know* what an impersonator is. I just didn't see any impersonator," she persisted.

Corrie broke out in a grin from ear to ear, "I understand."

"You understand what?" Rosa turned to her.

"Mama, Skunk saw Elvis! The real Elvis!" Corrie exclaimed.

Quickly I turned in the seat, "No! Nope, nope, that's not true. Corrie, it's time to change the subject. I saw an impersonator, I told him you were a huge fan and he signed the program. Period. End of story." I could feel my face flush and a light sheen of sweat on my forehead.

Wally wasn't any help. He was sitting there with a goofy grin on his face, thoroughly enjoying my squirming.

"Shut up," I mumbled.

Were we ever going to get to Jacksonville?

Chapter Twenty-Three

We finally made it, detour and all. It was hot and humid in Jacksonville. The palm trees drooped heavy fronds exhausted by the relentless heat. Everything sweltered under the late afternoon sun. Citrus groves scented the air with a salt air undertone. I found myself breathing deeply. It smelled so warm, fresh, and intoxicating. This was the first time I had ever seen a large body of water; my mouth fell open and my stomach tightened. It was so beautiful!

"What do you think, Red?" Wally asked behind a grin.

"It's beautiful!" I answered.

"That's not even the ocean, babe. Just wait," he said as though he was responsible for this breathtaking beauty.

"Are we almost there?" Corrie whined from the backseat.

The guy who lives in our GPS was busy giving directions and finally said our destination was on the left. Jacksonville Memorial Park was an expanse of green grass, water walkways, and then my breath caught in my chest. A sculpture of a sphere with a winged figure atop it was so beautiful against the backdrop of blue water with gentle whitecaps, it took my breath, quite literally, away. To my delight, Wally steered the car to the access parking lot. The car no sooner stopped and doors were flying open and Rosa, Corrie, Spirit, and Wally tumbled out, stretching backs and legs. Wally took that manly look-around and yawned. I couldn't take my eyes off the sculpture.

Wally leaned in, "You comin', Red?" he asked.

I dumbly nodded and opened my door. The air that hit me was soft, warm, fragrant, and just a bit of a chill coming off the water. Not enough I would need my hoodie but enough to tell me we were close to open water. It suddenly occurred to me: I had never seen the ocean. Never really thought about it but now that we were so close, I regretted having lived so many years not seeing it. I felt kindred with the softly undulating water and the secrets it held.

"Do you need to call Adrian?" he asked.

"Umm...yeah..." I still could not quit looking at the statue. I must have sounded dreamy and disoriented as I told her where we were. She said she was about ten minutes away and would be there shortly. I told her we would be at the sculpture of the ball and the angel. She laughed and said she knew what I meant. Rosa, Corrie, and Spirit were already out of sight, exploring and laughing like a couple of foals out for the first time in spring. Wally and I were walking toward the sculpture.

It was even more beautiful close-up. I could see more of the details. The sphere was the earth, covered in water. It was called Spiritualized Life. What I thought was an angel was the spirit of youth. It memorialized the young men and women who had given their lives in WW1. The plaque read:

While striving to make a composition visualizing this, I found a poem by Alan Seeger, a soldier- victim of the war.

At once I saw the typical spirit of the boys who went overseas – saw with their eyes a world in the insane grip of greed and ambition, caught in the ceaseless swirl of selfishness, hate and covetousness, ever struggling against submergence.

I saw these boys giving up their homes, sweethearts, wives and mothers to go overseas and through the supreme sacrifice make secure the happiness and safety of their loved ones.

With this vivid picture in mind, I constructed a sphere to represent the world, engirdled with masses of swirling water typifying the chaotic earth forces.

In this surging mass of waters, I shaped human figures, all striving to rise above this flood, struggling for mere existence.

Last, surmounting these swirling waters, with their human freight, I placed the winged figure of Youth, representative of spiritual life, the spirit of these boys which was the spirit of victory.

Immortality attained not through death, but deeds; not a victory of brute force, but of spirit.

This figure of Youth Sacrificed wears his crown of laurels won.
He holds aloft an olive branch, the emblem of peace.
**Created by Charles Adrian Pillars 1894'

I felt Wally's hand on my waist. I turned to him with tears in my eyes. I knew these boys. I knew whether they found peace or not. I knew how some of them died and how innocence in all of them died. I felt wounded to my very soul.

"I think Adrian is here," he said softly.

I turned to see a slender middle-aged woman walking toward us. She wore denim capris, sandals, and a sleeveless top. Her arms and legs were a golden brown, eyes hidden by large dark sunglasses and a wide-brimmed straw hat atop her head. She smiled showing perfect teeth and waved. Wally smiled back and returned the wave. As she approached us, I noticed her fingernails and toenails were painted a pretty coral. To be honest, I felt like a hulk.

We made introductions and small talk.

"I'm sorry but can I see the quilt?" she asked.

"Yes!" I said and led her back to the car. I dug around until I located the cardboard box. I opened it and showed her the quilt safely protected by a thick plastic case.

"It's beautiful!" she breathed. I had to agree. Even though it had hardly left my sight for the past couple of months, it still took my breath away when I saw it. Maybe because I knew what it took to get it to this point at this time, seventy-five years later.

Adrian looked up at me, "As I mentioned on the phone, Grandma Leah has dementia. She's in assisted living close by but I kind of felt I needed to try to prepare you."

She led us to a park bench. She removed her hat and fanned herself with it. "It's hot today. Well, it's hot every day but we have a storm brewing and it just makes the humidity nearly unbearable."

I smiled. It felt good to me. Wally was an expert at small talk, I just sat like a lump on a log, smiling and nodding and shaking my head at what I hoped, were appropriate pauses.

"Yesterday, she was completely out of her head. She was obsessed with her mother. She kept telling me to get out because her mom was coming to pick her up. I asked her why I had to get out and she said because I wasn't a Jew," she gave a little laugh but I could hear the pain just below the surface. "Apparently, when she was very small, she was only allowed to play with other Jewish children."

"I would imagine it was part of their culture," Wally offered.

"I can't imagine what her early life was like. She didn't talk about it a lot as I was growing up," she nodded. Inside my head I was thinking, *forget her early life. You have no idea what her mother went through to get this heirloom to you.*

"Anyway, if she's talking crazy when we get there, just let her go. I never correct her. I just let her say whatever pops into her head. Her memory of her earlier years is much clearer than her memory of ten minutes ago," Adrian said sadly.

"I understand," I said and laid my hand on her arm. My stomach knotted again as I fought to hold back tears. I was turning into a real softie and it just aggravated the hell out of me.

The assisted living facility was upscale living at its best. We passed through the guarded gate and were greeted by green, manicured lawns, immaculate sidewalks, cheerful flowers, and waving palm trees. Several residents were out walking small dogs, geriatric power walking, sitting on discreetly placed benches, and one older lady was trying her best to get her cat to walk on a leash. By the way, the cat was winning. All in all, a very nice, protected neighborhood.

Adrian went to a door and knocked. A lady opened the door and gave her a hug.

"Geiselle, these are my friends I called you about. Probably, Wally, Rosa, and her daughter, Corrie."

Everyone smiled and shook hands.

"How is she today?" Adrian asked.

Geiselle shook her head, "She's not having one of her good days. She refuses to eat and when I tried to help her dress, she bit me!"

"Oh! I'm so sorry!" Adrian gasped.

Corrie quickly excused herself saying she would walk Spirit.

"Put the harness and leash on him," I reminded her.

As for me, I wasn't so sure I wanted to visit with this crazy old lady that may or may not bite me in the process. I was sorely tempted to just give Geiselle the quilt and get the hell out of there.

"She doesn't mean it, Adrian, you know that. Poor dear doesn't understand what's happening to her and I think, she gets frustrated," Geiselle was saying as she led us to a living room.

Everything was bright and sunny in the room. The walls were a soft yellow and the sheer curtains at the window were a breezy white. The furniture was dark wicker with fluffy dark green cushions. A tall metal sculpture of a flamingo sat in front of the window and prints of palm trees and beaches were carefully arranged on the walls. I was bringing up the rear of our group, not in any hurry to meet this woman who was given to fits of rage.

"Miss Leah? You have company today!" Geiselle said cheerfully. Leah frowned at her care companion irritably. "Oh, now, it's your granddaughter, Adrian and some friends of hers."

"Go away," the old woman glowered.

"Miss Leah, they have a gift for you. Isn't that nice? They came a long way just to give it to you," Geiselle tried another tactic.

"I don't want any damned gift. I don't know these people. They're trying to poison me!" she insisted.

Geiselle looked over her shoulder and motioned me to step forward. Oh my. Oh my. I did not want to do this but I did. I stepped from behind Wally and taking a deep breath, I smiled .

She had a halo of thin white hair, thin skin with large brown age spots, and wore a lavender pantsuit with a brightly colored floral shell beneath. A medical alert necklace hung from her neck.

Leah looked at me, blinked, looked at me again. "Mama?"

I looked around and realized I was the one she was addressing.

"Oh, Mama!" she cried and threw up her arms so she could hug me. "I've missed you so much!"

Helplessly, I looked to Geiselle who was standing there dumbfounded and the others were decidedly uncomfortable.

Adrian finally came to my rescue, "Honey, that's not…"

I put my hand out to stop her from finishing. "Hello, darling girl. You're just as beautiful as ever," I smiled.

She grabbed my hands and led me to sit beside her on the wicker settee. "I don't know who all these people are, Mama. Should I ask them to leave?"

I was really having to think fast, it was exhausting. "No, Leah, I think it's nice they came to see you. You must mind your manners when entertaining guests though, right?"

"I'm sorry, Mama, of course, you're right," Leah said sheepishly. She looked at the little knot of people and smiled. "May I offer you some lemonade?"

Everyone just shook their head, afraid to break the spell. Corrie slipped in, leaving Spirit to cool in the kitchenette. Leah's eyes stopped at Corrie. She invited her to join us on the sofa.

"Mama, can you believe how much Maria has grown? She is beautiful still though, isn't she?" Leah said proudly.

Geiselle leaned into Wally and Rosa, "Maria was Miss Leah's great-granddaughter. She died of bone cancer when she was twelve. She seems to think this is some kind of reunion. Fascinating."

Adrian was very quiet and quietly left the room.

I remembered the quilt and tried to steer Leah's attention back to me. "Leah, I have something for you," I said not taking my eyes off her. I laid the package on her lap. She looked at it and cocked her head.

"What is it?" she asked.

"Would you like me to help you open the package?" I offered. I broke the seal and opened the plastic bag. As I began to pull the quilt out, tears ran down her cheeks. She looked up at me.

"My wedding quilt?" she trembled.

"Yes, my love, it's your wedding quilt," I said softly.

She gathered it to her face and cried.

Well, it was safe to say, there wasn't a dry eye in the room. I leaned in and kissed her on the cheek. She was fingering each pink rosebud, every leaf in the garland, the stitches that spelled the names of all the grandmothers who had passed it from daughter to daughter.

I looked up at Geiselle and nodded that it was time to go.

"Leah, I have to go now. Please, enjoy this quilt and I'm so sorry it took so long to get it to you," I said softly.

She looked up at me through tear puddled eyes, "I love you, Mama. Thank you. Will you come visit me again?"

I didn't know how much she would retain so I simply said, "I'll try."

Outside, I looked for Adrian and finally spotted her sitting on a bench beneath a large shade tree. I walked over and sat beside her.

"Thank you," she whispered.

"It was an honor to present it to her," I replied. "Are you okay?"

She nodded afraid to trust her voice.

"I admire you," I said. "Dementia is such a cruel disease. You've been so good to her. If she knew what was happening to her, I know she would be very proud of you, Adrian."

Her chin quivered, "I know she can't help it. I know I'm not part of her world anymore but I come to see her every day. I eat supper with her every night. I tend to her and constantly tell her I love her. Yet…"

"I know," I said softly.

"She remembers people in her yesterdays and not me," she finally sobbed.

I thought for a minute. I'm used to dealing with the dead. I'm unaccustomed to dealing with the living and the complexities of human emotion.

"Adrian, I'm not going to pretend I know much about this type of disease. You know, what thoughts they have or why, but I do believe that somewhere, stored away in a place just for you, she knows exactly who you are and I believe she loves you more than she's probably ever been able to say."

Adrian pulled a tissue out of her pocket and swiped her nose, "Thank you, Probably. I guess sometimes I need to hear that."

I put my arm around her shoulders and hugged her. "You know what I would do, if I were you?"

She shook her head still looking at the sidewalk.

"I'd go in and make a fuss over the quilt. After all, I believe you're next in line to receive it," I said with a smile. "She cried when I gave it to her. I think she's been waiting all these years to get it."

Adrian smiled, "You will never know just what a gift you've given to our family...to her especially. Thank you."

I went to the car, put my sunglasses on, and told Wally it was time to go. I couldn't help one last look as Adrian opened the door and disappeared inside. Vesta and Jacob followed her. Maybe Leah really did see her mother.

Chapter Twenty-Four

We decided to stay another couple of days. The days were just too beautiful, the air just too intoxicating, to leave just yet. Besides, I was emotionally drained. Fully spent. At least the look of pure, untainted love and joy on Leah's face helped to ease the sting of the nightmare. I lived a complicated life. I found myself wondering if I ever got dementia, what memories would I relive over and over? It's a sobering thought. Anyway, we got rooms at a very nice hotel located right on the beach. We could look out and see the Atlantic coastline.

Corrie couldn't wait to put her bathing suit on and hit the sand. I didn't bring a swimsuit. I didn't even own one but I did have the presence of mind to bring shorts and a tank top. I pulled my hair back into a ponytail, plopped on my sunglasses, and followed Corrie out. Wally and Rosa were getting things settled in the rooms.

We sat on the sand feeling the heat warm our bottoms and watched people playing with their dogs in the surf. Corrie wanted to go into the water and I hesitantly said okay but I was going with her. The sheer vast expanse of the ocean made me dizzy. The waves sucked at my shins and the wet sand shifted beneath my feet. My heart started racing. I felt out of control. I felt so small and insignificant in the face of such magnitude. Corrie was splashing and jumping each wave that came in. I was losing my balance. I tried to call for her but nothing would penetrate the crashing sound of water. I felt my knees buckle, I felt myself falling into the water, I tasted the saltiness, I felt the wave rush up my nose, and then all went black.

When I came to, a man was leaning over me. He was deeply tanned and wore red lifeguard swim trunks. "You okay, Miss?" his face swam before me.

"Yeah, peachy," I mumbled. I sounded like I had a mouth full of rocks.

"Here, drink some of this water," he said holding a water bottle to my lips.

"I feel stupid, not thirsty," I moaned.

"Nothing stupid about passing out," he said.

Wally came running up, out of breath, and spraying sand. "What happened? Are you okay, Red?" he panted on the verge of hysterics.

"I'm fine," I said feeling the strength return to my legs. "I just got too hot."

The lifeguard looked at Wally, "I'm guessing you two know each other."

"She's my fiancé," Wally said with a smile, "If she doesn't kill herself first."

For the first time, I noticed the crowd of people standing around me. They were starting to lose interest since I hadn't been attacked by a shark or drowned or something equally grotesque.

"Help me up," I said holding my hand up to Wally. "Where's Corrie?"

Corrie was nowhere to be found. Panic gripped my heart as I scrambled to my feet. "Wally! Where's Corrie? She was playing in the water!"

"Calm down, Red, I'm sure she's somewhere around here," Wally said nervously.

"Who's Corrie?" the lifeguard asked.

"A twelve-year-old girl that was with me!" my heart was racing to the point I was afraid I was going to pass out again.

The lifeguard immediately started questioning the remaining onlookers, inquiring if they recalled seeing a young girl with me.

"Corrie!" I screamed. Sweat was running down my face. "Corrie!"

Wally looked at the beach, the lifeguard looked at the water.

"Here, Red, here, look, she's coming with Rosa," Wally said turning me to see Corrie and Rosa trying to run in the sand.

I ran meeting them and nearly toppled Corrie as I embraced her.

She squashed against my wet belly and hugged me back.

"I went to get Mom. I didn't know what else to do!" she sobbed.

The crowd was once again disappointed there would be no added drama and drifted away murmuring to each other.

"I've had enough beach for today," I said still shaking. "I'm just wanting to go lay down for a while."

Wally smiled and took my hand, "I think that's an excellent idea. I can keep an eye on you better in the room."

I swatted at him as we headed toward the hotel. Rosa and Corrie stayed behind to enjoy the beach.

Later that night, I stepped out onto the balcony. The moon was high and full. It reflected on the waves and I could hear the crash and boom as they hit the sand. A slight breeze kissed my face. I watched people down in the tidewaters looking for something. A small fire burned with some of the people sitting on towels and laughing. I quietly went back into the room and dressed.

On the beach, I pulled my hoodie closer and began to walk in the darkness. It wasn't totally dark because the moon was full and gave everything a silver tint. I drifted away from the activity and found myself alone. There was a break wall and the waves crashed against it rising several feet in the air. It looked like Neptune was throwing diamonds in the moonlight. I sat close by and just felt the power of the waves reverberate against my pulse.

"Please, help me."

My skin crawled. I looked around but I didn't see anyone. Perhaps between the waves and my imagination, I only thought I heard something. A little uneasy now, I settled in once again. But I felt tense, no longer relaxed.

"Please, help me."

"Is someone there?" I called. The waves crashed and sucked at the sand.

I heard someone crying.

"I can't see you! Can you come to me?"

"Please, help me."

I stumbled off the rocks and tried to look around the surrounding area. The crying continued. It was so damned dark I couldn't see a thing. The shadows were blacker than black. I stepped on things I could not identify. I felt water squish in my shoes.

"Where are you?" I called. Had someone fallen? Were they hurt and praying someone would find them?

"Please, help me!" the voice was more urgent.

I waded out into the water desperately trying to see if someone was in the water. I ran along the ebb tide, sand getting into my shoes. It felt like I was running on shards of glass. It seemed no matter how far I ran, the voice was just out of reach. I began to cry in frustration.

"I can't find you! Where are you?" I screamed.

I waded further into the surf. "I'm coming but I don't know where you are!"

I looked down and screamed. Corrie's face looked up at me from under the water. Her hair swirled and wafted with the waves, her eyes open and unseeing.

"Oh, God! Oh, God! Corrie, what are you doing out here?" I frantically tried to reach under the water for her. Water splashed in my face as I groped and clawed to reach her.

"Miss? Are you okay?" I heard a voice but I didn't trust anything around me.

"Miss? Can I help you?" a man said approaching me carefully.

"Please, help me! Corrie is under the water and I can't reach her!" I panted. I clawed at the water trying to go deeper and deeper. Something large and black flew over my head, I could feel the wind of its wings graze me.

The man came into the water with me.

"Please, help me get her out of the water," I sobbed.

"Get who out of the water?" he asked.

"Corrie!"

He stood beside me and looked into the water. He looked back at me. "Miss, there's no one in the water."

I looked and she was gone.

"She was there! Maybe the waves pulled her out to deeper water!" I was terrified.

"Miss, come here and sit down," he said gently.

"No! We have to save her!" I screamed as he pulled me out of the water.

"Shhhhh…it's okay. I promise," he whispered.

I looked at him wildly. He sat me on the rocks of the break and then sat beside me.

"I don't understand," I cried shaking my head. "She was calling for help and I couldn't find her."

"Have you ever heard of Misery Shallows?" he asked.

I shook my head.

"Well, legend has it that many years ago a young woman stood on this very beach waiting for her true love to come in from fishing. His body washed up right here on this beach. She was so overcome with grief that she threw herself in the water and drowned so she could be with her love forever," he said. "People have been known to hear her call for help. You must have heard her calling."

I gave him a snide look, "Do not patronize me. I don't believe in fairy tales."

"Maybe it's a fairy tale or maybe not," he nodded. "All I know is that in this very spot, people have sworn they heard her calling."

"It sounded so real," I whispered.

He nodded his understanding.

"And who are you? Why are you out here in the dark?" I turned on him.

He laughed. "I'm Cooper and I live in a beach house just down the way. On nights with a full moon, I come down here to see if I can find the distraught maiden. I think I did find her tonight, even if it wasn't particularly the one I was looking for."

I couldn't help it, I smiled at him.

"How about I walk you home?" he said standing.

"Thanks but I'll be okay," I said as I looked one last time across the restless ocean. How many secrets did that black water hold? How many did it greedily hang on to, unwilling to return them to the land of the living?

"Thank you, Cooper. Thanks for coming by when you did," I said and I meant it.

"You sure you'll be okay?" he asked.

"Yeah. I just want to go home. It isn't that far away," I said as I turned and started walking back toward the hotel. As I turned to wave at Cooper, he was gone.

The next morning, I woke to a stomach that was sore and disagreeable. I started to get out of bed and bolted for the bathroom. I vomited up everything but my toenails. It woke Wally. He shuffled into the bathroom just as I was rinsing my mouth.

"Hey! What's wrong?" he asked alarmed.

"I don't know. I guess I swallowed too much seawater yesterday. I just want to lay down for a little while," I said, omitting my walk on the beach last night.

I lay in bed with my head throbbing and my stomach churning. Wally sat on the edge of the bed and brushed my hair out of my face.

"You're sweating, Red. Could you be getting sick?" he asked.

"I don't feel flu sick, just sick," I said though it took a great deal of effort.

"How about I call room service and have them bring up some tea and toast?" he suggested.

I nodded not at all sure tea and toast would make a difference.

He called in the order and as he hung up, there was a knock on the door. I heard hushed voices; I didn't have the strength to open my eyes. They left. No doubt Corrie and Rosa came to go to breakfast with us.

Room service came quickly and while Wally received it and tipped the server, I struggled to sit up in bed. The nausea was coming in waves now but didn't seem to threaten to come out my mouth. As I nibbled on the toast and sipped the hot tea, I began to feel much better. Wally was having a bagel with cream cheese and a fruit cup. I snagged a strawberry and popped it into my mouth.

"You seem to be feeling better," he laughed. "You know, I think when we get home you should see a doctor."

"I don't like doctors," I pouted.

"You might be having some sugar issues though. If you are, we need to fix it," he said.

He was right, of course. I didn't like the thought of something being out of whack in my body but I couldn't go on passing out and throwing up like it was no big deal.

"Oh! I almost forgot to tell you. I had the weirdest thing happen last night," I said draining my cup. He raised an eyebrow. "I went for a walk along the beach. I ended up at one of the breaks and heard someone calling for help."

"Wait. What? You went for a walk or you had a dream you went for a walk?" he said with scrunched brow.

"No, I went for a walk. It was so beautiful with the full moon and everything, I just couldn't resist," not fully understanding why he looked so irritated.

"Okay, when you finish your story, we're gonna need to revisit this," he said as he lay his spoon down.

I shook my head. "Anyway, as I was sitting on the rocks, I heard someone calling out. 'Please help me'. I kept trying to find them but it was so dark I couldn't see anything. They just kept calling and calling. I thought maybe someone was injured and couldn't get out of the water..."

"You are NOT going to tell me you went into the water, are you?" he practically yelled.

"Wally! Was I supposed to just let someone drown?" I yelled back. His jaw set hard.

"Anyway, I waded out...just a little bit, wasn't even up to my knees...and I saw someone under the water!" the fear that squeezed my heart last night came back with the memory.

"You're kidding? You saved someone from drowning?" now he was impressed.

"Well, not exactly. I was seeing..." I decided against telling him it was Corrie I saw under the water, "someone. I kept trying to reach them and it seemed they were just out of reach."

"Please, tell me you did not dive in after them," he groaned.

"No, no, I did not dive in after them but this guy shows up," I continued.

"Guy? What guy?" he was starting to sound pathetic and it occurred to me that perhaps I shouldn't share so much of my strange life.

"No, he lived close by. He said I was in Misery Shallows and he told this story about a young couple who...well, she was waiting for him to come in from fishing but he drowned and she was so distraught that she went into the water and drowned herself so they could be together forever. Quite romantic in a tragic kind of way, don't you think?"

He was speechless. Just sitting there with his mouth hanging open. I took my finger and tipped his chin to close it.

"Anyway, he offered to walk me back here but I said no," I finished rather lamely.

"Misery Shallows, huh?" he asked as he stacked the plates to set outside the door.

"Yeah, weird, right?" I asked. I felt like I was in trouble. I really, really felt like I was in trouble. "Oh! And he said his name was Cooper!" I exclaimed hoping that made it less sinister sounding.

"Okay, first of all, I guess I'm going to have to get used to crap like this. Secondly, even though I know you can take care of yourself, let's make a ground rule that you don't go meandering in the dark alone. And thirdly…"

I looked at him expectantly.

"I guess I shouldn't have made it sound like a long list. You feeling better?" he got up and pulled on a pair of jeans.

"Yeah," I said sheepishly. "Would you like to see Misery Shallows? In spite of the legend, it does seem like a neat spot."

"Sure, sure, I'd like that," he said. He smiled but it didn't show in his eyes.

We gathered up Spirit, Rosa, and Corrie and set out for the walk to the break. In daylight, it didn't seem so scary. Seaweed washed up on the beach. Corrie was collecting shells and little bits of driftwood. Spirit bounded after the waves and tried to bite them. When we got to the break, I saw little tidepools. Corrie was chasing tiny sand crabs and little long-legged birds ran after the waves and pecked at the sand, only to run away from the water when it returned to shore.

As we sat on the rocks enjoying the view, we saw dolphins playing far out to sea. They jumped, swam, and flipped. We laughed and I thought I'd never seen anything so beautiful in my life.

"That guy, Cooper, said he lived right along here in a beach house. I'd like to go say thank you for helping me last night," I said. In truth, I hoped that when Wally saw how nice Cooper was, maybe he wouldn't be so mad at me.

We stood up and wandered further down the beach. We finally saw a house. It looked rather dated and in ill repair. Maybe it wasn't such a good idea to bring Wally here. Too late now, I thought to myself. We walked up the overgrown path to the porch of the house. The door hung drunkenly on its hinges. The window screens long gone and hung in shreds. I stepped up and knocked on the door. There didn't seem to be anyone at home. The door opened under my knocking.

"Hello? Cooper?" I leaned in slightly.

Sand coated the floor. A broken chair lay in the corner. Cobwebs and spiders were the only residents I could see. There were no footprints in the sand.

"Maybe there's another house close by," I said uncertainly. We turned to go back to the beach.

A man was standing on the sand with a fishing pole. He turned to look at us.

"Mornin'" he said.

"Good morning. Having any luck this morning?" Wally asked.

"Nah. Storm's brewing. Thought it might bring in some of the smaller fish but guess they're staying out this morning," he said. "You folks on vacation?"

"Yeah, we're just here for a couple of days," I answered. "You from around here?"

"Born and raised," he answered.

"You probably know just about everyone around here, I guess," I said.

"Pretty much," he answered throwing out his line again.

"You ever hear of Misery Shallows?" I asked.

"Misery Shallows? Sure, I reckon everyone around here knows about that place," he was looking at me strangely.

"Yeah, I ended up there last night," I said to keep the conversation going.

"Uh-huh," he was staring straight ahead.

"Well, what can you tell me about the legend?" I asked.

He was silent, throwing the line out, reeling it back in, then throwing it out again. I didn't understand why he was being so weird and I didn't like the way it made me feel.

"Folks say it was a woman who found her lover drowned on the beach and then drowned herself. They say you can hear her callin' out for help on nights of a full moon. Tourists love that story," he said.

"But that's not what really happened?" Rosa asked.

"Nah," he said.

"What really happened?" I asked. He seemed so reluctant to talk about it.

"A young girl was murdered down there," he said.

"Murdered?" Wally and I said in unison.

"Yeah. It's been several years. They found her in the shallows. 'Bout nine or ten years old. Arrested some homeless beach bum. I heard he died in prison. There's a special code of honor in prison, I guess. They don't take kindly to child killers. As for folks hearin' her cry for help…well, maybe, maybe not," he explained.

"That's horrible!" I exclaimed. "I mean, about the little girl, not that he died in prison."

"Yeah, for years the name Cooper was whispered behind his family's back. None too kindly, I might add. They ended up movin' away when they sent him upstate. It was a tragic event," he said.

I felt the hairs on my arms stand up. I dare not look at Wally. The little girl I saw under the water wasn't Corrie but a murdered little girl. I didn't get saved by a kind man but rather visited by the spirit of a killer. Was he protecting his deadly deed?

All I know is that I couldn't get away from there fast enough.

Chapter Twenty-Five

If I had a noble heart, I should have tried to help the little girl find Rest. I was a coward, I left her there calling for the help that would never come. I never spoke of it again. When Wally brought it up, I just said it was one of my vivid dreams. I didn't want to talk about it. I didn't want to think about it. I didn't want to feel responsible for her.

Once we were home and life began to take on a normal feel again, I still felt off. I lost my appetite, I felt tired and wrung out. Wally kept pestering me about making an appointment with a doctor until I finally gave in and decided to go, if for nothing else than to shut him up.

Dr. Day was a kindly, old man. Rosa sang his praises so I figured that was as good as anyone. I could get a check-up, no harm in that. He poked, prodded, and asked endless questions. I answered as well as I could. When he asked if I was sexually active, I said no and felt my face flush. I wasn't in the habit of discussing such personal issues, much less with a stranger, even if it was a doctor. Then I remembered the night of the nightmare.

"Wait a minute, I did…you know, only one time," I said.

He nodded. "I think we'll do a pregnancy test, just in case," he said.

That was ridiculous! I told him that wasn't necessary. After all, it was only one time, seriously, one time.

I finally gave in and peed in a cup and let them take some blood. I don't know why I was so embarrassed but I was and it was pissing me off. When it was all over with, I just wanted to go home. This is why I hated doctors. They were always looking for something, anything. I suspiciously thought it was to justify charging a second mortgage and once they got their hooks in you, you just kept going back and going back.

At home, Wally met me at the door.

"They couldn't find anything wrong with me," I announced as I breezed past him and went into the kitchen for some apple juice.

"So...everything's okay?" he asked.

"Yep, they took blood, and poked, and prodded, I feel like a friggin' pin cushion," I said discreetly veering away from the pregnancy test.

"Well, that's good news! Thank you for going, Red," he said and gave me a peck on the cheek.

Later that afternoon, Dr. Day's office called. They wanted me to come back the next day. Wally raised an eyebrow.

"I'm going with you," he said as I hung up.

"I don't think that's necessary," I said.

"Okay but I'm still going," he persisted.

"Whatever," I said. "I'm going to take a shower."

The next morning, Wally and I sat in the waiting room and a nurse came to the door and called my name. Several people swiveled their heads to see who in the world would be named Probably Magic. I smiled at them as Wally and I followed her. Instead of going into an exam room, she took us to Dr. Day's office. We sat there not saying anything waiting for him to join us.

"You know everything's okay, right?" I said breaking the silence.

"Yeah, I know," he said for my benefit.

Dr. Day came in and sat at his desk.

He stuck his hand out to Wally, "Hi. I'm Dr. Day."

Wally shook his hand, "I'm Wally, Probably's fiancé."

Dr. Day smiled. "Well, we got the results back on your tests."

"And?" I prodded. I'm not much of one for theatrics. Let's get this over with.

"I'll want to do an exam but Probably...and Wally, you're going to have a baby!"

I couldn't have been more stunned if someone suddenly kicked me in the stomach.

Wally's mouth was hanging open.

"You did have sex, right? Even if it was only one time," Dr. Day said with sparkling eyes.

"Yes, but there has to be a mistake, Doctor. There's just no way," I was spluttering.

"Apparently, there is," he smiled. "Is this happy news? I can't tell."

Wally came to life, "Yes! Yes! It's wonderful news!"

I gawked at him dumbly.

"Red! We're going to be a mom and dad!" he chortled.

"I don't have to listen to this," I huffed and I swear to you, I got up and stormed out of the office, through the waiting room, and out to the car. I have never heard anything so ridiculous in all my life! It had to be a mistake! One time! One freakin' time! You know what? I don't want to sit in the stupid car. I got out and started walking. I wasn't even sure I was going in the right direction; I just knew I had to be out in the open. I was so livid, so angry, so shocked, I was power walking.

All at once, I remembered the nightmare. Brendore was threatening to take my child. At the time, there was no child but now there was. This thought made me weak in the knees. I sat on the curb with my back against a light pole. Now there is a child. What on earth was I going to do with a child? I wasn't ready. I didn't even like kids, except for Corrie but then she always was older than her age. How could I protect it? Or because of ignorance, had I promised the child to Brendore in exchange for Wally? How could I choose between the two?

A car pulled up and stopped. I heard the car door slam and footsteps approach me. I looked up into the face of Wally and burst into tears. Cars swerved around our car, horns honking, and one motorist slowed, lowered his window and shouted, "Get out of the damned road, Dumbass!" We ignored them all.

"Red, it's going to be okay," he said.

"How? I don't know anything about babies. I don't even know if I like babies. How can I be a mom when I don't feel like a mom?" I moaned.

"It will all fall into place. Red, I love you," he said kissing me on top my head. "Do you love me?"

My heart broke, "Oh, yes, Wally, I love you more than life itself!"

He lay a hand on my belly, "Well, this little person growing inside you is the best of both of us. This baby is someone, another little human, made by us and our love for each other."

I shook my head, "That's really cheesy, Wally. You don't understand."

"Then help me understand," he said.

"Wally, I deal with dead people and demons and worlds different from ours. I have visions, and dreams, and dangerous missions. How can I bring an innocent baby into all that? Hell! I worried about bringing YOU into all this!" I wanted to tell him about the dream but I just couldn't bring myself to do it. As long as I didn't talk about it, maybe it would just stay a dream. "How can I protect our family from all the dangers even as we struggle to survive?"

"Red, I don't have all the answers but one thing I know beyond a shadow of a doubt. We'll figure it all out together, just like we've always done. As long as we face our strange lives together, we'll be okay," he said softly. He made it sound so possible.

"We should move the car, Dumbass," I smiled.

He laughed and helped me stand. Before getting in the car, he held me close and kissed me in a long, tender kiss. The honking horns turned to happy honks and cheers.

When we got home, I was famished. As I went about making us bologna sandwiches, chips, and applesauce I really did feel a little surer of myself and even allowed myself to be happy. As we ate lunch we talked about all things baby, cribs, clothing, what kind of diapers, and all that stuff that new mothers are supposed to be excited about.

"I don't want to tell anyone yet," I blurted out of the blue.

"Huh?" he stopped mid-bite.

Well, now that it was out there floating around in the universe, I didn't know what to do with it. "I mean, I want some time to get used to the idea. You know, wrap my head around it."

"That makes sense," Wally agreed. "It's a lot for both of us. Sooner or later though, people are gonna know something's up when you get fat and your boobs get bigger."

"Oh, my gosh! I forgot all about that! See? I'm not ready for a baby!" I exclaimed.

Wally laughed.

That night after we cleaned the kitchen, I felt about ready to melt into the floor. I went into Wally's room and removed his pillows from the bed.

"What cha doin', Red?" he asked.

"I'm moving you into my room," I said as I tossed the pillows on the bed. "You like right or left?"

"Ummm…are you sure?" he asked scratching his head.

I put my hands on my hips and looked at the bed, "Well, one thing's for sure. I can't get *more* pregnant."

He laughed and pulled me down on the bed with him. "I thought this day would never come."

Spirit jumped on the bed looking forward to a good wrestle session. Wally put his arms around the wolf's neck. "Guess what, buddy? You're going to have a little brother or sister!"

In true Spirit fashion, he cocked his head and stared at us. It seemed he was mulling over what he'd been told, then lay next to me with his head on my belly.

"I love my boys," I said and dang it, I could feel tears. Did pregnancy make one weepy? If so, I hated that part.

Chapter Twenty-Six

Well, knowing I was pregnant didn't make the morning sickness go away. Wally was a sweetheart though and brought me crackers and apple juice every morning so I could manage to get out of bed in the first place.

Miss Vera came overbearing her wonderful, magical cinnamon rolls. As soon as she walked through the door and I caught the first delicious whiff, I turned heel and ran into the bathroom and vomited.

She was quite hurt. Wally shrugged his shoulders and said, "I think she's got a little stomach bug."

She traded the cinnamon rolls for chicken noodle soup. I thanked her and she stood right there until I sat at the table and began to eat it.

"Mmmmm..." I said hoping she would leave before another incident.

"You look flushed, sweetheart," she cooed. "I think perhaps you need some of Aunt Jo's tea."

"NO!" I yelled entirely too loud. She took a step back. "I mean...I think this soup will do the trick. See? My stomach is better already." I began to eat one spoonful after another.

She was flustered. "I'm so sorry, dear. You've just always loved my cinnamon rolls and..."

"Oh, I do!" I assured her. "Just give me a couple of days to get my sea legs back and I'll gorge myself on them." Inwardly, I was thinking more like a couple of months. I didn't know what was in Aunt Jo's charmed tea and I didn't want anything foreign getting to 'little bug'.

Wally gently but firmly guided her out the door taking the basket of rolls from her. He winked at her, "I'm not sick."

"Brat," I said under my breath.

The soup really did taste good and it really did make me feel a little better. By afternoon, I was feeling somewhat like my old self. I did have a headache, though. I was worried about that stupid dream. I've never had one that stayed so long in my brain. That made me wonder if there was some message I was supposed to be getting.

"Let's go up in the mountains," I said. Late spring was my favorite time of year. The delicate wildflowers determined to bloom against all odds of the unpredictable mountain weather. The new babies just starting to explore their woodland home, the rivers and waterfalls swollen with melted snow and pop-up showers. Late May into early June, the most beautiful time for the mountains.

"Are you sure?" Wally asked.

"Why not? Exercise is good for me and Bug," I said.

"I guess so. Okay, I'll get the backpacks," he said. He turned around, "Bug?"

I laughed. "Well, we keep telling people I have a stomach bug so I figured, you know, Bug!"

Wally shook his head, "I don't know how to feel about our love child being called Bug."

I threw a dishtowel at him.

We were tramping along our favorite trail and even though it was pretty muddy, the leaf debris padded the ground. Spirit was delirious with all the new smells and was happy to run back and forth. He would disappear for a while and then he'd show up in front of us. If I didn't know better, I'd say he was keeping an eye on me.

I was getting a little winded so we decided to stop along a creek and have our granola bars and bottled water.

"Have you thought of names, other than Bug?" Wally asked me as he looked at the rushing creek.

"Names? Shouldn't we see what it is first?" I responded.

"Well, there's a fifty-fifty chance it will be either a boy or a girl," he acknowledged. "Maybe we should have some names in mind for either way."

"Gee, I haven't even thought of names," I admitted. "In fact, to be honest, I haven't thought much about the baby at all. Should I be?"

Wally played with a stick, "Honey, I'm not familiar with the intricacies of pregnant women. Maybe we can talk to the doctor and ask some questions."

"And let him know I'm totally stupid about something most women take for granted?" I said horrified.

"Well, what about Rosa? She had Corrie, maybe she can help you," he suggested.

"No. There's something keeping me from accepting this. I just don't know what," I lied. I knew full well what the problem was. I just didn't know what I was supposed to do about it.

All at once we heard a blood-curdling howl. It was joined by another and another.

"Where's Spirit?" I asked panicked.

"I don't know," Wally said standing to look into the dense forest.

The crescendo rose as more and more howls echoed through the forest. It was nerve wracking.

"Let's get the hell out of here," Wally said grabbing my hand and pulling me toward the trail.

"Spirit!" I called over my shoulder.

The howling continued. All I could think was that Spirit was a wolf too, he should be safe. Shouldn't he?

"Spirit!" I called again.

I could hear something crashing through the underbrush. I saw wolves begin to appear on the trail.

"Wally!" I screamed. "Do something!"

He just continued to pull me along with the wolves stalking us with heads down and hackles up. "Whatever you do, don't run."

"What? Of course, I'm gonna run!" I yelled.

"No! They'll see you as prey," he said.

The wolves were starting to close in on us. I could hear others beside us in the branches of the Rhododendron. I saw flashes of silver fur and once in a while, yellow eyes. I could hardly breathe. We came to the area where we had to climb a slight hill. Wally began to push me toward the incline.

"Go!" he yelled as he gave my bottom a shove.

"Wally!" I screamed my throat feeling like it was being ripped apart.

A large wolf charged and lunged for Wally. I was screaming and screaming. All at once, a large silver body rocketed out of the undergrowth and attacked the wolf, gaining a hold on its neck. The wolf gave a piercing cry and then returned the attack. Fur tumbled over fur, jaws snapping. A couple of other wolves joined the battle. There were yelps, growls, and guttural threats. Blood sprayed from ripping muzzles, drool dripped from razor sharp teeth, as they ripped and snarled in a frenzy.

I couldn't quit looking. Wally grabbed me and shoved me the rest of the way up the hill. A few of the wolves watched us, considered us, then went back to the carnage.

Once up the hill, we ran for the car. We dove inside and locked the doors. We were both shaking and in shock. I didn't know what to do or say or feel, except relief. We just sat there panting and then I started to cry. Wally did too. We held onto each other and bawled like a couple of little girls. I had to pee something fierce. I thought about Spirit and reached for the door handle.

"Where do you think you're going?" Wally asked holding me even tighter.

A black shadow slid over the car and the cawing of a crow made my skin crawl. It circled above us, cawing and cawing before flying deep into the forest.

"I'm going to go check on Spirit," I said firmly. I knew that was Brendore letting me know I was at his mercy. I was so angry I was shaking for a whole different reason.

"I'll go. You stay here," he said.

"Like hell I'm staying here!" I screeched.

"Red, think of…Bug," he said. "It's too dangerous."

He opened the door and stepped out. The howling had stopped. Squirrels were chattering, birds were singing, and woodpeckers played the trees like drums. I felt disoriented. Could this have been a vision? I hated not being able to trust anything in my life.

194

Chapter Twenty-Seven

It seemed Wally was gone a long time. I ventured toward a stand of large shrubbery and peed. I became worried and restless. I heard before I saw Wally carrying Spirit in his arms. He was struggling but refused to let loose of the two hundred seventy-pound wolf.

My heart hitched in my chest. I ran to help him carry Spirit. His fur was matted with blood. His eyes milky.

"Oh no, oh no, oh please no," I sobbed.

"I'm sorry, Red," Wally lay Spirit on the ground. Spirit sighed and then it was over.

I fell to my knees and wrapped my arms around his neck. I was the one howling now. Spirit had saved our lives at the expense of his own. I wouldn't let Wally touch him and I wouldn't let go of him. He had been my faithful companion for so long, I didn't know how I could go on without him. I remembered that tiny little pup stranded on the rocks in the river. When Animal Control took him away. When he defended me when I was hellbent on being stupid. My confidant, my best friend, the other half of my heart. No more romps in the woods, waking to him lying beside me, playing with Corrie, or treats from Miss Vera. Life felt as though it was over. And there was only one person to blame…Brendore. The anger started as an ember and slowly became an inferno.

Wally waited me out and eventually I helped him load Spirit into the cargo area. He seemed so huge, just lying there. In life, he was my companion, almost like a person instead of a wolf. I knew Brendore was responsible for this and I would have my revenge.

"You're strangely quiet, Red," Wally said as we approached our house.

"I'm sorry," I said absently.

We told Miss Vera what happened and she burst into tears. We decided to hold a funeral for him and buried him in the back of the property where he loved to run and play. Aunt Jo showed up, how or if she knew, I had no idea. She didn't cry openly but I knew her heart was breaking because she let me hold her as Wally lowered Spirit into the ground. We threw wildflowers on his body then covered him with dirt. Wally had made a cross out of scrap wood and said that would do until he could get something better. It seemed pretty fitting though. Spirit was a complicated soul. While part of him wanted to run with the wolves, the other part wanted his nice warm bed and treats from his favorite babysitter.

As we walked back to the house I turned to Wally, "Babe, I need to talk to Miss Vera and Aunt Jo. You mind going on home?"

He looked at me carefully, "Sure, okay. You alright?"

"No," I said simply, "But I do need to talk to the both of them. Thank you."

Miss Vera, Aunt Jo, and I sat at Miss Vera's kitchen table. I had just relayed the dream in which Brendore was forcing me to make a decision between our child or Wally. I saw Aunt Jo start to tremble. I also told them about the girl in the water when we were in Florida. I knew that was a threat, regardless of what the local stories were. My skin crawled when I thought about the murderer who offered to walk me home. That was extremely dangerous and I didn't even realize it.

"Then the incident today," I continued. "That was Brendore. I know it was because he made himself known and he was very pleased with himself."

"Oh, Probably," Miss Vera said with tears puddled in her eyes. "We have to do something! He's had it out for you since day one!"

"I know," I agreed, "But it has to end at some point."

Aunt Jo's head snapped up, "How?"

I took a deep breath. Once the words were spoken out loud, there would be no turning back. No excuses. I wanted to speak but the words were stuck. Miss Vera and Aunt Jo looked at me with concern.

"I want to have a final showdown with Brendore," I said.

"NO! Absolutely not!" Miss Vera said with a force I'd never heard before.

"Probably, I understand how you feel but demons cannot be killed. You can't kill something that isn't alive in the first place," Aunt Jo tried to reason with me.

"Maybe I can't kill him but I can send him back to hell where he belongs," there, it was out. The no turning back point.

"And how do you plan to do that?" Miss Vera was visibly crying now.

"I don't know yet but I'll figure something out," I said.

We sat there just staring at the table, Miss Vera sniffing and Aunt Jo tapping her booted foot against the chair leg. No one knew what to say.

"I have an idea," Aunt Jo said.

"Jo, do not encourage this insanity. I'm not ready to lose Probably and Wally," Miss Vera looked pretty angry.

"One thing I've learned about this kid is that when she gets something in her head, nothing will stop her. I say, let's help her and try to make it as safe as possible," Aunt Jo defended me and right at that moment, I could have kissed her.

"Now, hysterics aside, what did you have in mind?" she turned back to me.

"Well, I know I will have to confront him on his turf," I began.

"You want to go into the realm again?" Miss Vera said wide-eyed.

"Yes," I nodded.

"I'll go with you," Aunt Jo said.

"Oh, Jo! You can't! If you go over, you can never come back! What is wrong with everyone? Have you all gone crazy?" Miss Vera turned to me, "Probably, I know losing Spirit is traumatic but, honey, it's just his physical body that's gone. His sweet spirit is still alive and well. He'll just show up in another form when he's needed. It isn't the end of him."

I hadn't thought of it that way and while it did make me feel a little better, still, he should have never died in the first place.

"Aunt Jo, I can't ask you to do that. This is something I'll have to do myself. The war is between me and Brendore. The fewer people involved, the safer it will be," I said shaking my head while I declined her offer.

"I'm sorry. Did you think I was asking your permission?" she said with flashing eyes.

Miss Vera rose from her chair, "I don't understand any of this. I don't understand how you could jeopardize the life of an unborn baby and yourself! You're getting married! Think of what it would do to Wally!"

"What unborn baby? I never said anything about being pregnant!" I panicked.

Miss Vera just glared at me. I remembered when we first met and how she knew things about me I never told her. I should have known I wouldn't be able to keep this from her. I took her hand and sat her back down, "Miss Vera, Brendore knows I would never be able to choose between Wally and our child. This is a cruel position he has put me in and he's savoring my struggle and my fear. If I can send him to hell, then Wally is safer, I'm safer, and Bug is safer."

They both looked at me, "Bug?"

I laughed, "Yeah, we kept saying I had a stomach bug and since we don't know if it's a boy or girl, I call it Bug."

"That works," Aunt Jo said amicably.

"I don't like this. I don't like it all," Miss Vera was shaking her head.

"It will be okay. I promise," I said. "There's just one more thing. No one can tell Wally."

When the silence became unbearable, I said I would talk with them again and we would get our plan in action.

I felt very awkward walking across the backyard to my cottage. Big words coming from someone whose knees still knocked together every time a spirit showed itself. I would find the courage though.

I didn't sleep well that night. I could play scenarios in my head but I had no idea what I was up against and I certainly had no idea just how I was going to destroy Brendore's hold on the afterlife. I just kept thinking about him telling me I had to make a choice. Perhaps he knew I had no choice and enjoyed seeing me struggle and worry about the outcome. I missed Spirit and it only fueled the fire in my belly. Every time I thought about those wolves attacking us, I just knew Brendore was tightening the noose. I had walked those trails hundreds of times in the six years I'd lived here. I knew those mountains like the back of my hand. Never once, not even a hint, of trouble from any of the wildlife, except those foul-tempered squirrels who liked to throw acorns at me. That was a battle for another day.

Daylight crept into the bedroom. Wally snorted and flopped on his side away from the window. Looking at him sleeping with no thought of the danger we were in, made my heartache. I instinctively put my hand on my belly. There was a bit of a pooch but I could still hide it. I was going to have to act fast before I became too heavy with the pregnancy and perhaps too protective of it. The more I thought about it, the more I knew just how true it was, that I had no choice. Perhaps that was his plan all the while. He knew he was pushing me into a corner where I would have to fight him. He was pretty confident he was going to win. I had to make sure he was wrong.

I decided that I would face off with him on his turf. He was a shape-shifter and an influencer in the world of the living. In the Realm, he was what he was. The trade-off was that in the Realm, I had no powers to use as weapons. It was strictly a David vs. Goliath situation.

"Did you sleep at all?" I heard a sleepy mumble as Wally lay his hand on my back.

"No," I said.

"Come here," he whispered.

I scooted over and he held me in a tight embrace. "I love you," he sighed in my ear.

I smiled but I felt like crying.

Chapter Twenty-Eight

I knew I needed to talk to Wally. I needed to get rid of him so I could try to get myself killed. I didn't think he would see the merit in that plan. I couldn't let him know something was up and to be honest, I had yet to master the poker face.

He asked if I would like to go into town with him but I begged off telling him I was really tired and kind of out of sorts. Would he mind going without me? Once he was gone, I wandered around the house. It felt incredibly small, with no extra room for all these huge, stomping, intruding thoughts in my head. We would most likely have to find another home, a little larger that could have a nursery. Kids still started out in nurseries, didn't they? It was amazing how little I knew about babies. It was equally amazing that I lacked any motivation to learn. Maybe once all this was settled, one way or another, I'd feel differently. I just didn't know. Could be, I didn't have what it took and I was the last person in the history of the world that should be having a baby.

I went to my closet and reached up to the top shelf and retrieved the glass box that held the red marble. I turned it over in my hands. Otis Smoot was a magician who was sweet, inadequate as a magician, tender-hearted, and always apologetic. He also accidentally blew up the theater where he was performing, killing all the people in the building including himself. He told me about getting seven marbles from a famous magician to help him achieve greatness. "They hold unspeakable power, so use them wisely," the master magician had told him. Poor Otis did not realize just what he held in his hands. My mission was to rescue the people in the audience that night imprisoned by Brendore in the Third Realm. Otis was a hero that day. Not the way he'd always dreamed of being a hero but a hero in the strictest sense of the word. I ended up with the seventh magic marble and you'd better believe I put that bad boy in this glass case to forever contain its power and to protect the world from ever knowing just what a simple orb of red glass was capable of.

I had a feeling this marble would now be a key component to my survival and the survival of the people I loved and cherished. I had no idea how I would use it. I had no idea just what, if anything, it could do. Pretty pathetic that my entire plan for survival depended on a glass marble. Now, I had to figure out a way to get Wally far away from me for his own safety, without him knowing I was sending him far away for his own safety. Try as I may, I couldn't come up with a good excuse that wouldn't lead to a million questions, some hurt feelings, and a door slam or two. The more I thought on it, the more I thought that maybe I should just come clean. He would either understand or he wouldn't. Since I didn't have a clue what else to do, I decided the sooner the better.

When Wally got home from the grocery store, I kind of hovered over him, trying to string some words together that made sense. He was kind of quiet too as he put the yogurt and milk in the fridge and cereal in the cabinet.

I took a deep breath and he turned around to me.

I need to talk with you," we both said at the exact same moment.

We laughed a little and I said, "Jinx! You owe me a Cadillac!"

He said, "I don't know if that's a good thing or not. You go first."

I panicked. "No, why don't you?"

He looked down at the floor, at the coffee maker on the counter, puffed out a breath, and said, "Well, okay. See, the thing is…well, you know Bug…Geez, this is hard."

"Wally, what's going on?" my belly tightened. Was he going to tell me he didn't want to be…didn't want Bug? Maybe now that we were to become parents, maybe he didn't want the life I was chained to.

"Okay, here's the thing. I don't want to tell mom and dad that we're getting married AND making them grandparents over the phone," he blurted out. "That's something I think should be done in person. That's a lot to take in and…well…you know how Mom can be."

"Well, oddly enough, I agree. I think that's a good idea," I could have cried with relief.

"Yeah, well, the other part of that is that I think I should tell them…you know, alone.'"

"Okay," I said.

"Really?"

"Well, yeah, although I think they will be thrilled that it's good news and not that I'm trying to get you killed again," I laughed.

"You'll be okay while I'm gone?" he asked.

Ah, the sticking point. I couldn't get my voice to work so I just nodded my head.

"I hope…I mean…Babe, I don't mean to hurt your feelings," he said stepping toward me.

I do not know what made me do it, I've thought about it time and time again, and I don't know what was going through my mind but as he reached for me, I stepped away from him!

"Ah, shit, Red! I *did* hurt your feelings!" he exclaimed.

"No!" I nearly shouted, "No, you didn't, honestly and truly, you didn't. I don't know why I stepped back. Bad timing, maybe?"

To show there were no hard feelings, I gave him a hug. "Go see your family. Help them get used to the idea of being called Grandma and Grandpa. I understand and I agree with you. Your mom doesn't care all that much for me."

"Oh, she does, she just takes a while to warm up to people," he said into my hair.

"Especially women who always seem to land you in the hospital," and we laughed. "When do you think you'll go?"

"Well, I kind of thought I'd leave this afternoon. You think staying a couple of days would be okay? Can you stay out of trouble that long? Oh, for crying out loud, look who I'm talking to!" he laughed.

You have no idea, I thought to myself.

I hung up the phone. Adrian had called to tell us Miss Leah passed away this morning. She said it was peaceful and that she was holding the wedding quilt. I gave her my condolences. We talked for a while and eventually, it was time to say goodbye. She thanked us profusely for making the long trip to Florida to give her grandmother the quilt. I was glad she had it but it was also tinged with a bit of sadness.

"I'm going over to Miss Vera's for a while. Let me know when you're ready for lunch," I said. He looked at me a little cock-eyed but I pretended not to notice.

I knocked on Miss Vera's door and let myself in. As usual, she was at the stove fixing eggs for breakfast. Cherry Turnovers already sat on the table accompanied by a plate of bacon. My stomach rumbled. It seemed I was always hungry lately. Miss Vera sat me down and poured a glass of orange juice. When the eggs were done, she put some on my plate and then fixed a plate for Wally.

"I'll be right back," she said as she hurried out the door.

It seemed I could feel the tension in the air, or maybe just a universal instability. Whatever it was, I didn't like it one bit. I finished my breakfast by the time she got back. She busied herself with cleaning up the kitchen. She tried to make small talk, asking how the garden was doing, what was ready to harvest, and my, oh, my how fast the summer was passing. I was never good at small talk.

"We need to talk, Miss Vera," I said grabbing her wrist as buzzed by me.

She nodded and sat at the table with me.

"I've been giving this a lot of thought," she said.

I waited for further information but she remained silent.

"And?" I finally coaxed her.

"Probably, so much is changing. It makes me dizzy when I think of that wild-haired girl who showed up on my doorstep a few years ago and how much everything has changed. I felt we were living in perfect times. I knew better. I knew the only thing that never changes is that things always change. I'm having trouble accepting that," she said softly.

"I know," I said, "But if I don't do this, Miss Vera, none of us will be safe."

"I don't know what that means, Probably," she said. "What is *'this'*? What exactly are you going to do? You can't face someone like Brendore and not have a plan."

She was right, of course. I needed to have it worked out in my head before I went in with guns blazing. I also didn't know what would become of the underworld once he had been vanquished. How's that for confidence? I already believed I would win. I had to win. There was no other option on the table.

"Well, don't you have some of those heebie jeebie rocks like the last time I went into the Realm?" I asked grasping at straws.

"They aren't heebie jeebie rocks, as you say. And they helped you navigate through the Realm, not destroy it," she said irritably. "You don't seem to understand that this world and that world do not overlap. You can't take the energies of the living world and take it with you to the dead world."

"Miss Vera, I simply cannot believe there is no way to function in the Realm. I've been there. I've interacted with it. I'm familiar with its illusions and deceptions. We just need to find a way to use those things to our advantage," I argued.

She sat thinking about that for a moment. "Maybe…"

I softly said, "The marble."

"What?" she looked up at me.

"The marble from Mr. Magnificent. I still have it." I took it from my jeans pocket and lay it on the table.

"What can that marble do?" she asked.

"Whatever we want it to," I said with a smile. I began to feel excitement as the shapes, colors, and swirls began to congeal into a plan. "Miss Vera, I will be much stronger than Brendore because I have something he will never have. I have the force of love, the shield of encouragement, the energy of life, and the marble. I can carry all those things into the Realm with me."

"Probably, you know I love you but you just sound crazy now," she said. "I don't see how that's going to do any good. Think a moment, Brendore has been the Overlord for centuries. Centuries, Probably! You're not even making any sense," she was getting frustrated with me. I can't say as I blamed her. "Brendore has survived countless exorcisms.

I put my hand over hers and waited until she looked me in the eye, "But he has never had to survive against me…Red Probably Magic. I need you to trust me."

"Probably…" she started.

"Just…trust me," I repeated.

She didn't respond one way or the other but I do think she resigned herself to the fact there would be no changing my mind.

"Wally is leaving this afternoon to go back home and break the news to his parents about the wedding and the baby. We need to do this quickly. Can we be ready by tonight?" I asked.

Miss Vera's response was to burst into tears and flee the room.

I just sat there for a moment. Was I supposed to leave? Should I wait for her to compose herself? I stood and put the tea kettle on instead. I noticed my hands were slightly shaking.

Chapter Twenty-Nine

Miss Vera was upset over the whole chain of events. I felt horrible. I was disrupting so many lives. I was demanding they be loyal to me and yet I was acting like a loose cannon. I felt that if they had been with me in that dream, they would have understood. I put the marble back in my pocket and took her the cup of tea I prepared. For the first time, I wished I had some of Aunt Jo's Charmed Tea. Miss Vera could use it about now.

    Once I got her calmed down, I wandered back home to help Wally get ready for his trip to his parent's house. I felt I was made of cement, each step heavier than the next. Dear sweet, Wally. What would he come home to? A family or a funeral? The emotions were steel cords in my chest. Stretched taut and to the breaking point. He looked at me so innocently. We had such completely different perspectives of the simple act of him visiting his family. Yet, it was best we keep those perspectives unshared.

    I kissed him. I felt the heat rise in me as I wanted to feel him closer to me. I wanted to remember his man scent, his tense muscles, his sweet breath. I wanted to take the very love he had for me into this battle. I think I understood why so many couples made love right before they deployed. They wanted to carry with them the reason they went to battle. They wanted that love to sustain them. We ended up making love. It wasn't the desperate coupling to dispel the coldness of death this time. It was sweet and slow and savored.

We kissed all the way to the front door. I gave him one last kiss, watched him get in the Tahoe, back out of the drive, and wave. Then he was gone. I watched him until he turned on Shelton Street and out of sight. I turned back into the house. It was a small cottage that I had loved for the past six years. Now, no Spirit, no Wally, no giggling Miss Vera, it felt cavernous. I suppose I was waiting to see what happened next.

I fixed a can of New England Clam Chowder for dinner. As I stirred while it heated, I heard the front door open. I instinctively braced myself.

"Hey! You home?" I heard Aunt Jo call. I smiled.

"In the kitchen!" I called back. I heard her boots clomp down the hall and toward the kitchen.

"What cha' got goin' there?" she asked sniffing the air.

"Clam chowder, want some?" I offered.

She wrinkled her nose.

"Fine. I have some of those butter cookies you like up in the cabinet. I swear, it's a wonder you have any teeth in your head," I scolded. "How can anybody consume so much sugar?"

"It's what gives me such a sweet disposition," she retorted as she rummaged for the cookies.

That made me laugh. It felt good.

Next came Miss Vera. She wasn't okay but she was trying, I have to give her that.

"You want some clam chowder?" I asked her.

"Out of a can?" she shuddered and shook her head no.

"Sorry," I said as I poured some in a bowl for myself.

"I see no reason to prolong this," she said as she sat at the table. "Unless I can try to talk you out of this one last time…"

I blew on the spoon of chowder to cool it, "Nope." I sounded a lot braver than I felt, or did I sound a lot crazier than I felt? I may have voted for the crazy version. Sometimes I felt like we were three little girls playing dress-up and chasing dragons. But this was real and that made me sad. When you pretend, you always win. Reality wasn't as kind.

We talked about my decision yet again. I was to the point of just being plain stubborn. As I said before, once those words were out in the universe, there would be no turning back. I heard a knock on the door and cocked an eyebrow. "Were you expecting someone else?"

Miss Vera stood to answer the door. I heard her talking to someone and I heard a familiar voice. Miss Vera and Dr. Leslie Turnbow came into the kitchen. I choked on the last spoonful of chowder. As I was spluttering and spraying chowder across the table, Dr. Turnbow gave me a disgusted look.

"I understand you want to go into the Realm and fight Brendore," he said without preamble.

I nodded my head.

"So...I'm curious, were you born stupid or did you have to craft it?" he asked.

"Hey!" I protested.

He just shook his head. "You have no idea what you're doing. You have no defenses. You don't even know where you're going in the Realm and you have absolutely, positively no regard for those you leave behind. Now, tell me, Miss Sarangoski, does that sound smart or stupid to you?"

"Why are you being so mean to me?" I whined. I didn't mean to whine; it just came out.

"Miss, this is nothing compared to what Brendore will do to you," he said softly. "He will make you doubt yourself. He will make you question your strength. He will appeal to your instincts to protect those you love. He will prey on your insecurities. If you should survive, which is highly unlikely, you will never be the same," he was staring straight into my soul. "So, I ask you, were you born stupid?"

I thought I would feel anger at the insult but instead, I realized I was indeed stupid. I have always doubted myself. From the time Peter Euclid showed up to the bizarre mission of Claire Roman. And yet…yet I had completed each mission. I had granted those poor, restless souls Rest. I had stolen from Brendore, I had played on Brendore's weaknesses, I had won battle after battle against him. Now, it was time for the war.

"Dr. Turnbow, you may be right. I may be stupid but I believe I am stupid for all the right reasons. I may not be able to win this war but it would be stupid not to try. It would be stupid to back down and let Brendore continue to destroy families, to consume innocent souls, to reign terror only people like you and I can see. It would be stupid to make him think he really is invincible. You're right. I have no defenses, no grand battle plan, no armies on my side, I have nothing but the right reasons to guide me. Sometimes, people mistake faith for stupid. I have faith I will succeed. I envision sending Brendore to hell. I have a burning desire to banish him from this world and send him back to the world he deserves. I don't know how I'm going to do it but not doing it isn't even an option for me," I said with a surprisingly steady voice.

His face never wavered from the dark glare. I stared right back into his eyes. Slowly, I saw a corner of his mouth begin to turn up. His eyes softened. He patted my hand and smiled.

"Let's get started then, shall we?" he said. I saw a new respect for me in his eyes.

"I'm going with her," Aunt Jo said as she pushed away from the cookie container.

Dr. Turnbow looked at me.

"Give me a minute, please?" I asked him. I took Aunt Jo by the arm and took her into the living room.

"You're not going," I said.

"I AM going," she replied.

"No. You're not going. This is something only I can do," I said.

"Probably, you'll need me!" she protested.

"I will always need you," I said, "but I need you here. I need you to be with me and Wally. I need you to watch over Bug like you've always watched over me. It's much more important that I have you here when I return."

"*If* you return," she pouted.

All I could do was smile at her.

"It's going to be okay. I will carry what's good and right in the world with me. Haven't you read any fairy tales at all? Good always overcomes evil," I said jokingly. "Please, if ever I needed you, it's now and I need you to stay here. Promise me."

She didn't like it, not one little bit but eventually, she nodded.

I gave her a hug and whispered against that insane aviator hat, "I love you. Thank you."

Dr. Turnbow and Miss Vera came into the living room.

"Are we ready?" he asked.

I hugged Miss Vera. She hugged me back tightly. I saw tears in her eyes. "It's going to be okay," I whispered to her.

For good measure, I hugged Aunt Jo. No words were needed.

I turned to Dr. Turnbow and nodded. I sat on the couch as I had before. He took his finger and started making small, tight circles on the bridge of my nose. His eyes sparkled like glitter. I felt myself falling but I wasn't afraid this time. I was resigned.

Chapter Thirty

I was in the black room with the river of souls racing beside me. I didn't look at them this time. It seemed I reached the light at the end rather quickly. I stepped through the threshold into the white room. I could clearly see the giant gold and teal bird named Lin-Lin guarding the Realm.

"Why are you back?" he asked grumpily.

"Gonna pick a fight with a demon," I said simply.

"Why would you do that?" he asked.

"Because I figured I didn't have anything else to do and it sounded like fun," I answered.

"You're a smartass," he said but I could tell he was smiling. His smile slipped from his beak. "This will not be like your last visit, Red Probably Magic. He is expecting you. He will not play games this time."

I drew a deep breath, "I know but then neither will I."

"Are you absolutely certain you want to pursue this foolish quest of yours?" he squinted one emerald eye at me.

"Yes," I said.

"Very well," he said and produced the golden key. He hesitated and then inserted it. The door opened.

As I stepped through, I remembered the Panteras, dog-like creatures with rows of razor-sharp teeth and a poisonous bite. They didn't like loud noises. Would they remember me and realize I was basically harmless albeit very noisy? My eyes hurt from straining to see all around me at once. Things could appear and disappear in a nano-second. Things could shapeshift from harmless to deadly. This world could kill you in an instant or lull you into a false sense of security with its beauty.

As I was picking my way down the pale path, it suddenly occurred to me, I had no idea where I was going. Did I just wait for Brendore to show himself? Did I call out to him? Would I know when he was near or would I unknowingly walk into his trap? Well, now I felt stupid and that marble in my pocket seemed pretty stupid too. I reached around and made sure it was still there.

I was approaching the forest. I remembered the deep, almost black, emerald color. There were shadows everywhere. Some shadows moved, some did not. It was hard to know if it was friend or foe stalking me. I saw the beautiful vines wrapping around the trees, their bright neon red flowers beckoning to me. The Vine of Souls. Oh, yeah, I remembered the Vine of Souls. It danged near killed me last time. I walked a wide berth around it. I figured I'd walked enough for now and decided I'd take a break. I sat on a boulder at the base of a tree and took in my surroundings. While some things seemed familiar to me, other things did not. Kind of like being away from your hometown for many, many years and then coming back. While it was all familiar, much had changed and you had to find your way around the new changes.

I really missed the sounds of the forest. Even though I had not been back to the mountains since…since That Time, I still loved the activity, the busyness, the life that carried on whether I was there or not. Here, there was nothing. No sounds, no natural breeze, no growing greenery, everything was stoic and sterile. It was enough to make your gut tighten.

I began to think that Brendore was purposely staying away. He probably thought if he waited long enough, I'd start to doubt myself, my resolve would weaken, perhaps I'd just give up and …

A blinding pain speared me in the middle of my back. Air escaped my lungs as I dropped to my knees. As I struggled to stand, another jolt smacked my chest, and this time I saw stars. It sent me reeling backward, striking my head on a rock. I shook my head trying to clear it. From the corner of my eye, I saw a blinding flash. I rolled on the ground to a stand of trees and hid behind them. The tops of the trees exploded, sparks rained down on me burning my scalp and face. I could smell burned flesh

"What the hell?" I shouted.

A throaty, rumble of laughter filled the air around me. I chanced a look and lo and behold, Brendore came strolling through the forest as though the briars and limbs and uneven ground phased him not one bit. He was laughing, his eyes glowing red.

"Word is, you think you've come to dethrone me, you puny little pissant," he roared.

I wasn't prepared for such a vicious attack. I'd just kind of figured we'd banter first like we always did. He meant to stop me, for good.

"There's no thinking to it, Brendore, I WILL destroy you!" I shouted from behind my tree. I peeked around to see where he was and I didn't see him. As I sighed in relief and took a deep breath, I turned and he was right in my face. His breath had a stench of ripe roadkill. Involuntarily, I gasped.

His clawed finger traced my jawline. We were too close for me to make any move at all. I stood as still as I could. The claw trailed down my neck, over my collarbone, between my breasts, and stopped. He cocked his head and pinned me with his stare. He threw back his head and laughed. "So, you bring the child to me!"

I didn't say anything. He started to lay his scaly hand on my belly.

"Touch me one more time, you ugly scum sucker, and I will die killing you," I said in a low voice.

He howled with laughter and whirled into the air turning into a crow and flying away.

I put my back against the tree and slid down gasping for breath. If he had wanted to kill me, he would have done so right then. He wanted to play with me like a cat with a mouse. My right shoulder burned with a white-hot intensity that made it feel almost cold. My back felt bruised. I thought of Wally coming home and Miss Vera telling him I had died unexpectantly. That caused my stomach to heave but I refused to give in to it. I needed to empty my mind of everything but the danger at hand. I could afford no distractions. The war had begun. I would either wake up in my living room or I would be locked in this world forever.

When I felt my breathing regulate, I stood up and surveyed the forest. It was quiet. I didn't trust my footsteps. Unknown, unseen dangers lurked on every side of me. *Don't give in to the fear,* I told myself. Remember what Miss Vera said, *our greatest danger is fear. Fear is a dragon to be slayed for our survival.* Convincing myself I was much stronger than my gut told me I felt, I continued on the path.

I heard a noise in the darkness surrounding me. I stopped and listened. I'd heard that sound before. My heart began to race. Brendore's hellhounds, the Manoucks, were coming! I looked frantically for a tree to climb. I needed to be out of their reach. I scooted up the nearest tree and stood on the lower branches just as they broke through the underbrush. They were snarling and snapping their jaws, eyes glowing blood red, saliva hanging in glistening strands. They jumped at the tree trying to reach me. I was trapped. Maybe this wasn't such a good idea.

I saw vines snaking up the next tree. The Vine of Souls. If I got near it, it would entangle me squeezing the life out of me, feeding on my blood. I couldn't chance touching it. I had an idea. I broke off a large limb and used it to poke the vine. It attached to the limb. I let it circle the limb a good way and threw it among the Manoucks. It immediately began to attack the hell hounds. They were yelping as it wrapped their muzzles, tightened around their chest, and snaked into their nostrils. It was a gruesome scene but after a short while, the Manoucks were devoured by the vine and they disappeared from sight. Now, I had to figure out how to get down without touching the vine.

The tree next to me, the one that had the vine, offered me a limb. I didn't know about the wisdom of this but I couldn't see a long list of options at this point. I finally grabbed the branch and it pulled me over to the tree next to it and so on. I was being passed around by these trees until I was out of the danger zone from the vine. I thanked them and began my journey once again.

I was getting tired and in a great deal of pain but I knew I couldn't chance resting. I pushed on through the darkness just hoping at some point I would emerge into the light. It was exhausting trying to find my footing, being hyper-aware of my surroundings, and being on guard in case Brendore had more tricks up his sleeve.

"Come," I heard a voice sigh. I stopped and looked around me. "Come."

"Who's there?" I called.

"I will keep you safe," it whispered.

"Yeah, I don't see that happening," I said to the nothingness.

"Do you remember Mother Tree?"

I did remember Mother Tree. When I was here before, I was injured by a Manouck. Mother Tree gave me her life force. She withered and died but I lived.

"Yes, I do remember Mother Tree," I replied.

"Then come. You can rest safely," it said.

"How do I know you're not another one of Brendore's tricks?" I asked.

"Because you are here to destroy him. To destroy him would be to return to the beauty of the forest. We have been imprisoned for so long. We will help you."

Well, they DID save me from the Manouck attack and the Vine of Souls. I slowly took a step off the path. Truth be told, I could use a friend in the Realm.

"Come."

As soon as my foot went off the path, a sense of dread filled me. I knew in my heart of hearts this was exactly the wrong thing to do. I quickly pulled my foot back. Quick as a bullet, my brain told me Mother Tree had come to me, the tree who passed me safely past the vines came to me. Never once had a sea fairy, a tree, or anything else ever make me get off the path. It occurred to me this path, though not a safe zone, was a path of safety of sorts. I began to run. I ran as fast as I could, tripping over roots and stones and whipping limbs.

Breathless, my legs weak and threatening to buckle, I came up short. I was at the River of Sorrows. On the other side was Brendore's domain. I sat panting and holding my side as pain throbbed so hard it hurt my heart. I felt a slight movement. Surprised, I looked at my belly. I felt it again. Bug was urging me on. Fine but I had to shed some tears first.

Chapter Thirty-One

The River of Sorrows rushed by me carrying the restless lost souls. I was feeling dizzy, tired, injured, and helpless. In hindsight, I should have thought this out a little better but no, not me! Let's just bust right on in with no plan whatsoever! Red Probably Magic liked to fly by the seat of her pants. Well, that was going to get me killed. I stopped. Self-doubt. Hopelessness. That was the effect demons had on the living. I really had to watch that. The real problem at hand was how to get across the River of Sorrows.

Crossing the River of Sorrows would put me smack into Brendore's lair. It's where he feasted on the souls he captured. The prison where he tortured prisoners denied Rest. I would be at his mercy. All this aside, I knew I had to get across somehow. My back and my collarbone were stinging like fire. I took off the hoodie and saw burning holes where I'd been hit by Brendore's lightning bolts. I couldn't see the wounds but I could feel them. I dropped the hoodie into the river. A bridge appeared. I stepped back trying to reason just what that meant.

Another trap? I touched the railing and it felt solid enough. Maybe if I took a running start I could get across before anything had a chance to happen. The bridge began to fade. It was now or never. I closed my eyes and took a running go at it. I made it across just as it shimmered and disappeared. *Weird*, I thought to myself.

This was no time to think about the practicalities of such a feat. I was now in the inner sanctuary of Brendore, Demon Overlord of the Underworld. It was wide-open…nothingness. I saw a bobbing head in the distance. I walked cautiously toward it. As I walked, grass appeared with my footsteps. I saw a second movement. My heart started racing. There was something oddly familiar about those shapes.

I began to run. The grass was streaking now beneath my steps. The wide-open space began to fill with grass, wildflowers, and trees. I stopped short. I watched Corrie pick white flowers and sing a sweet unfamiliar song. Spirit romped around her. I began to hiccup sobs.

"Corrie!" I screamed. She looked up at me and waved. Spirit stood stock-still, tongue hanging out as he panted.

I began to run to them. "I'm coming, baby. Stay right there!"

She stood smiling as she waved.

Oh, my God! Why was she here? I stumbled but righted myself and kept running.

"Corrie!" I screamed. I saw a dark shadow slither across the clearing. Fear squeezed my heart. "Corrie! Run!"

She stood smiling and waving. I felt I wasn't getting any closer. The dark shadow grew, moving like a wave through the grass.

"Run!" I screamed until my throat was raw. The dark wave was right behind her. Spirit yelped and fell to the ground. Corrie smiled and the darkness swallowed her.

My knees buckled and I fell on my face. My nose gave a sickening crack and I felt blood begin to trickle before the flow. I scrambled upright. Brendore stood with Corrie in his arms. I couldn't catch my breath as the horror overcame me.

He was smiling and took a claw and raked it down her cheek. Rivulets of blood ran down her face. She struggled but her tiny body was no match for the demon.

"This is between you and me, Brendore!" I shouted. "What is it about you hiding behind old women and children? Do you think you're not strong enough to fight me on your own?" I was thoroughly pissed.

His smile slipped and he threw Corrie to the ground.

In no time, he had advanced to within inches of my face.

"You're always in such a hurry to die," he snarled.

"I haven't died yet!" I shouted at him.

With the back of his hand, he slapped me and my body flew several feet before landing near jagged rocks. I could already taste blood in my mouth. I got back on my feet. My nose was throbbing. I couldn't afford the time to wipe the blood away and so it flowed into my mouth and down my chin. My head ached and loudly echoed my racing heart.

"You fight like a girl," I taunted him. He sent one of his fireballs and I barely dodged in time.

"You want to fight me, yet you have no weapon," he said.

"I have no weapons you can *see*," I said with menace.

This made him consider just what that implied.

"I don't need to show off my power," I continued. "I don't need theatrics or tricks."

"Tough talk for a mere Walkie about to die," he laughed.

"So, take me on," I raised my hands and gestured for him to come to me.

He levitated a rock and hurled it at me. I didn't duck in time and it hit me in the forehead. Colors exploded inside my brain. For a few seconds, I couldn't see anything but colors. I felt blood begin to flow from the gash.

I gave a war cry and ran straight at him. He raised his palm and flicked his wrist. I felt I had been punched in the gut as I flew through the air. I refused to think about the baby and whether or not it could survive such a beating. I had no sooner stood on shaking legs when Brendore grabbed a handful of hair and swung me in a circle. I felt hair loosen from the scalp. He flung me against a tree. My body threatened to lose consciousness. I couldn't find the strength to stand. I struggled to my hands and knees shaking my throbbing head. I staggered to my feet. I could barely see him through the blood running into my eyes. My body wanted to collapse and just lay in the grass but I summoned all the strength I had left and faced him.

"Are we finished dancing yet?" I weakly tried to shout.

He took long strides until he was in my face again.

"Geez, Mac, get a breath mint!" I growled scrunching my nose.

He glared trembling with rage at me. "I'm tired of playing with you."

He disappeared. This couldn't be good.

I took advantage of his momentary absence to assess the damage to my body. My T-shirt had some pretty nasty tears in it. My forehead was bleeding, my scalp burned, my back felt broken, and my nose was swelling my nostrils shut, in short, I felt like death warmed over. I was curious as to what he was up to now. I couldn't let my guard down. I should really piss him off and go looking for him. Let him be the hunted for once.

When I saw him, my heart slammed into my chest. He brought reinforcements. There were demons of every size and shape marching behind him. He had a smug look on his face. This was an impossible situation. There was no way I could stand against an entire army of demons!

"Awww...did the little demon-wemon need some help?" I forced a laugh. I was in enough pain my stomach was queasy. I could only hope Bug was okay.

Brendore's hand shot out and grabbed me by the throat. His face was mottled with anger and hatred. I tried to cough but my windpipe was being crushed. My head felt like it was going to explode. I clawed at my back pocket for the marble but my shaking fingers couldn't find it. My eyes were about to pop out of my head. As though peering underwater, I saw Brendore laugh. Weakly I pulled at his hand but I did not have the strength to release his grip. He shook me viciously and threw me on the ground. I gasped for air and fell with a bone-jarring thud. Rocking back and forth I got on my hands and knees. I fell prone and rolled to my side. I tried again. My head weighed a thousand pounds. I found it difficult to raise it enough to give him a look that meant I wasn't about to give up no matter how much he beat me. I finally got to my feet. The whole world was swaying and I felt seasick.

"Submit to me, Red Probably Magic!" he roared.

"No," I croaked and spit blood.

He grabbed me by the hair and forced my face to his. "You are dying! Submit! Admit your defeat!"

I spat in his face. He shook me again with such force I felt my brain turn to mush. I was losing consciousness. He threw me away from him yet again and as I hit the ground, I heard a sickening crack in my shoulder. He was right, I was dying. I did not have the strength to stand again. I tried but my body would not obey my command. I lay on the ground bleeding and panting, rolling into a fetal position.

"*You must stand,*" I heard a voice in my head. "*You must not give up.*"

I shook my head trying to clear it. I tried to stand but I fell on my face. I tried again and failed.

"*Stand against him, Red Probably Magic. Find the inner strength to face him!*"

I began to cry, blood bubbled from my mouth. My eyes were swelling nearly shut. I finally managed to stand, weaving back and forth.

"It's over, Red Probably Magic," Brendore said softly.

"Probably," I heard a voice behind me. I whirled around, fists up.

Catalina stood beside me. From the tree line stepped Peter Euclid, Bob McCoy, Claire Roman, Rosa Hargate, LeLonna, Jacob and Vesta, Mr. Magnificent, all the restless souls I had helped over the past six years. I felt my chin quiver and my throat close. They formed a circle around me. Mr. Magnificent, aka Otis Smoot, walked to the center of the circle and stood with me. I reached in my back pocket and withdrew the marble. He smiled. Brendore had a smug smile. My little ragtag army against his deadly demons.

The last to arrive was a spirit with long flowing white-blonde hair. She wore robes of pale green that shimmered and sparkled, nearly translucent. She floated in the air and when she was above me, she dropped the robes on me. They enveloped me with warmth, strength, and resolve. I took a deep breath while I closed my eyes and felt life return to my battered body.

The circle of spirits, led by Catalina, began to chant:

Crux Sacra Sit Mihi Lux
Non Draco Sit Mihi Dux
Crux Sanctipatris
Vade Retro Satana: Nunquam Suade Mihi Vana
Sunt Mala Quae Libas
Ipse Venena Bibas

The chant gained volume as more and more of the spirits joined. I listened to it and watched Brendore's reaction.

"Stop! You're all so stupid! You cannot banish me!" he laughed and his army laughed with him. "The game is over. I'm tired of you, Red Probably Magic." He turned to his minions and shouted, "Kill them all!"

The chant wasn't working. He was right, a spirit could not kill him. As I listened more closely to the chant, the words formed in my brain. A spirit couldn't kill him but I could and I can't think of anything in my life that I wanted more than to see Brendore thrown through the gates of Hell. I held the marble in my hand and stepped outside the protective circle. I had my own smug smile.

"They may not be able to destroy you…" I said loudly, "But I can and I will!"

He started to rush me but as though there was a force field surrounding me, he was stopped. He commanded his army to advance.

As loudly as I could I began to chant in unison:
May the Holy Cross be a light unto me,
And may the Dragon never be my guide.
The cross of the Holy Father of Light.
Get behind me Satan; never suggest vain thoughts to me.
The cup you offer me is evil;

Drink the poison yourself!

Brendore's army began to turn to dust. Brendore stomped his feet and roared so fiercely, the sky trembled and the ground heaved. I kissed the marble and with every ounce of strength I had, I hurled it into his screaming maw. He screamed in pain. He beat his chest. He began to burn from within. I watched as he burned but I didn't stop chanting. He appeared to be melting, turning to glowing embers until nothing was left but a pile of black ash. They scattered like dust.

Chapter Thirty-Two

A bright light rolled in from the distance. In its wake, grass, wildflowers, and trees sprung up. Butterflies flitted from flower to flower. I stared in awe and amazement. As the light approached us, I saw hundreds of souls engulfed by it. These were the souls Brendore had imprisoned. Hundreds and hundreds willingly and joyfully stepped into it. Even the spirits who had fought with me, one by one, stepped into the light and vanished. I was having a hard time wrapping this beautiful scene around my brain. It was surreal.

Eventually, only Catalina and I stood in the pastoral clearing.

"What happened?" I asked her.

She turned and smiled at me, "You sent my father back to hell where he belongs."

"I did?" I said incredulously. "I really sent him back and not just away?"

"You did, Red Probably Magic," she laughed.

"Well, what happens now?" I asked.

She cocked her head and still smiling, "Now, the Realm will be what it was intended to be. A beautiful journey to Rest. Brendore, my father, leeched beauty, and happiness, and light from everything he touched. He's gone now. His hold has been broken."

"What about...I mean...what happens if another demon takes his place?" I asked.

"Well, we'll just have to make sure they don't," she replied.

I was thinking I wasn't so sure I could survive another battle such as this. Yet, this wasn't my world. I didn't have any say whatsoever about what happens in the Realm, BUT...

"Hey, aren't you a demon?" I said squinting my eyes at her.

"Yes. What are you thinking?" she asked giving me the stink eye.

I smiled at her, "Queen of the Underworld has a nice ring, don't you think?"

She laughed, "Does sound kinda nice, doesn't it? I like the way you think!"

I realized I was still wearing the green robes. I fingered the delicate fabric. It was such a pale green but shimmered and danced in the bright light.

"You should feel very honored," Catalina said softly.

"Oh, I do!" I said, "Who was she?"

Catalina smiled, "That was Mother Tree. How's your arm?"

I was puzzled why she should ask such a strange question then I realized all my injuries had healed. I felt those little gas bubbles in my belly again. Bug was okay!

"But Mother Tree gave me her life force. I watched her die," I said as I remembered the last time I was in the Realm. I had been attacked by a Manouck. I was dying when Mother Tree scooped me up into her branches and healed me. I watched as her leaves withered, curled, and fell to the ground until there was nothing left of her.

"Her spirit was freed when she gave you her life force," Catalina said. "Now, she can return to being Mother Tree to all living things."

"Probably, it's time to go home," I heard a voice in my head say.

Strange as it may seem, I was in no hurry to leave. It was beautiful here. Brendore no longer ruled the Realm. The robes shimmered, casting prisms around me, then slowly faded away.

"Okay. Just five more minutes," I answered the voice.

"Promise me you will reign fair and just," I said.

"Well, I am a demon, so there's that but I do promise I will not carry my father's legacy," she said.

"Fair enough," I laughed. "I guess it's time for me to go."

I felt a little dizzy. I closed my eyes to regain my equilibrium and when I opened them, I was staring into the eyes of Dr. Turnbow. I felt a little sad.

"I'm going to need a minute," I said. I took several deep breaths.

"Thank you," I said to Dr. Turnbow.

"I think the gratitude belongs to you," he smiled at me. He SMILED AT ME! "Do understand you haven't cleansed the afterlife. You've removed a threat but you haven't conquered the evil."

I nodded, "I understand but I think things will be better...at least for a little while."

He stood and gave me a little bow. He placed his hat on his head and vanished.

Miss Vera sat quietly.

"Soooo...what now?" I asked her.

She took a deep breath and put a smile on her face. "We have a wedding to prepare for!"

Great, I knew what that tone of voice meant. She would have me in frothy wedding dresses, shoes God never intended for human feet, and all those little details that seemed important to everyone but me. She lived for these moments. I couldn't help but giggle a little.

"That sounds good but you know what I really want right this minute?" I asked mischievously.

"What?"

"Something to eat. I'm starving! And a nice long nap," I said stifling a yawn.

"Of course!" she said jumping up and hurrying to the kitchen.

I lay my head against the back of the sofa and thought about what I had just been through. I wondered how much Miss Vera knew. She wasn't one for showing her hand too soon but she seemed different somehow. My eyes closed and I was fast asleep.

Chapter Thirty-Three

I never told Wally about the battle with Brendore. I felt it best we just accept things as they were and be grateful we were all still together. Miss Vera, Rosa, Corrie, and even Aunt Jo were excited about the wedding plans. I let them do as they will and to be honest, I felt like a Barbie doll.

Aunt Jo kept saying, "Good luck getting her to wear white!"

Miss Vera replying, "But it's her wedding! Brides wear white."

They were having fun though and I guess that made it all worth it. They had me try on filmy dresses, something called a sweetheart neckline, one was called a mermaid, then there was a strapless. I tried one on they called a Ball Gown with lots and lots of layers. I looked like a freakin' cupcake. I told them I didn't have enough boobs to hold up a strapless but they said it could be altered without any problem whatsoever. Every dress was white with long veils, short veils, and no veil at all. None of them took my breath away. It just didn't feel like me. But they were having fun so I willingly put dresses on, took dresses off, put other dresses on.

Wally was easy. He said, "Red, you just tell me where and when and I'll be there with a boutonniere in my lapel and a ring in my pocket."

We had to decide on a venue too. Since neither one of us was super religious, we went through several different ideas but none of them seem to really work for us. Summer was winding down it would be into fall before long. Bug had turned my baby bump into a baby mountain. So, the dress that fit last week didn't necessarily fit this week. It all seemed rather chaotic to me. I mean, all this fuss for just a couple of hours of ceremony.

One night there was a knock on the door and when I answered it, Rosa was standing there.

"Hey! Is everything okay?" I greeted her.

"Yeah, everything's fine I just... Well, I just get the feeling, you know, that you're not crazy about any of the dresses you've been trying on. Now, understand you're under no obligation but Corrie and I made you a dress. You want to see it? This... Well, Corrie and I just thought maybe this might be a little more your style." She handed me a rather large box.

I invited her in and we went into the living room where I opened the box. Inside was a very pale mint green, much like the robes from Mother Tree. Iridescent dragonflies dotted the outer layer which fell over a mint green satin dress. It was very filmy and what Miss Vera called an empire waist. It had thin straps over the shoulders with a cape attached that fell into a translucent train. It was the most beautiful thing I've ever seen.

"Oh Rosa, it's absolutely lovely!" I gasped.

"Go try it on!" she urged. "I mean...if you want to."

"Absolutely! Wait here, I'll be right out," I said and I felt like a little girl who always wanted to be a princess.

I went into my room and struggled into the dress. Being pregnant I didn't move as well as I used to. However, once I got it on, I couldn't quit looking at myself. Even without my hair and makeup done it was just breathtaking.

I walked out into the living room to show her. Miss Vera and Aunt Jo and Corrie were all waiting for me. There was a stunned silence and I figured maybe it wasn't what they had in mind for my wedding dress. Aunt Jo was the first one to say something.

"Now *that's* our Probably Magic!" she exclaimed. "Told you she wouldn't wear white!"

We heard Wally in the kitchen, and my cohorts yelled in unison, "Get out!"

We laughed and I didn't want to take the dress off. It was perfect. I strutted around and hugged Rosa.

"Thank you so much! It's the most beautiful wedding dress I've ever seen. And believe me, these past few weeks I have seen enough to last a lifetime!" I wished I could tell her why I thought it was so beautiful but I kept the Realm out of the world of the living. I offered cookies and tea and we sat laughing and talking about the wedding. I sat on the couch with my sneaker-clad feet on the coffee table and yards and yards of wedding dress swallowing any extra room.

Corrie kept looking at me. In fact, she was staring.

"You okay?" I asked her.

She nodded and averted her eyes but they strayed back to me again. I cocked my head at her.

"You don't look like Skunk," she finally said. "You look like a princess."

I smiled at her. I loved that girl so much! I hoped that if I have a daughter, she's just like this little girl staring at me.

"I don't know. Princess Skunk sounds pretty good. Don't you think?" I said with a grin.

We laughed and I figured I'd better change before I managed to ruin this beautiful confection of a dress.

"Have you decided where you're going to have it yet?" Rosa asked once I'd settled back in wearing my jeans and t-shirt.

I figured I'd throw my idea out there and see what kind of a reaction I got. "I want to have the ceremony in the mountains." I braced myself for all the objections.

"I think that makes perfect sense," Corrie said.

Everyone nodded but Miss Vera.

"Sweetie, you're pregnant and that's a long way up there. How could you hike all that way in a long dress and pregnant?" she asked.

"I think I'll be just fine," I said stubbornly. "Besides, exercise is good for me."

"We're coming into fall, you know. What about the weather?" she tried another approach.

"We'll have everyone bring a coat," I countered.

"What about snow? The mountains are unpredictable. We could have three feet of snow by then," she wasn't giving up.

"Then we'll use snowmobiles and snowshoes," I was kind of enjoying this back and forth. I would say, likely me more than her. She took a deep, deep sigh with her brow furrowed. I hugged her.

"Don't worry, Miss Vera, everything will be beautiful. Trust me," I whispered in her ear. I looked at this wonderful circle of women whom I was so proud to call my friends and said mischievously, "Unless we have it within the next couple of weeks."

There was a surprised silence. I smiled.

"Oh, I think we could pull that off," Aunt Jo said hesitantly.

Miss Vera turned and looked at her incredulously, "How? We haven't even finished making plans! What about the reception? What about the cake, the food, the rehearsal?"

Aunt Jo shrugged her shoulders, "We have a bride and a groom. We have witnesses and a venue. I think we have everything we need."

I laughed because these two women were so endearing, so opposite of one another, and so loved by me.

"I thought I would ask Uncle Dave to marry us," I said reaching for another cookie. I caught the look that passed over Aunt Jo's face.

"I don't think he's licensed for marriages," she said doubtfully.

"I bet he could get licensed really easy. After all, he has two weeks," I argued. "Aunt Jo, would you mind calling him and asking him?"

Oh, yeah, I was stirring the pot. She didn't know that I knew they had stayed in touch since the Claire Roman case.

Finally, she said she'd try but she wasn't making any promises. She didn't know when she would call him. Yeah, right. She was going to call him as soon as she left my house.

The afternoon passed with plenty of laughter and joking and planning. As I looked around me at the smiling faces, Bug kicked me hard in the ribs. I began to laugh. I was exhausted. Thankfully, Rosa noticed my fatigue and politely said it was time to leave. Everyone took the hint and soon the house was quiet once again. I went into the kitchen and found Wally sitting at the table reading a book. He looked up and smiled.

"Have fun?" he asked.

"I did! What a bunch of old hens, huh?" I said with a chuckle.

He smiled and nodded, "You look tired. You want to take a nap?"

"You know, I think I will. It's kind of late in the day but a nap sounds good," I admitted.

I lay on the bed thinking that in two weeks, three tops, I would wear that beautiful green dress, tromp through the woods, say some vows, and my life would be changed forever. That always made my heart beat a little faster. As much as I loved Wally, as much as we'd been through together, it still filled me with panic to think he would permanently be attached to me for the rest of my life...as I would be attached to his. Were we ready for that gigantic leap? How much would our lives change? Bug got the hiccups and I shifted to make us both more comfortable. We decided we didn't want to know the sex of Bug. We would just wait and be surprised together. I drifted into a happy, restful sleep. I'm not sure but I think I fell asleep smiling.

Something warm and fuzzy was tickling my nose. Wally needed to shave if he was wanting to do some nuzzling. A tongue slurped my nose and my eyes flew open. A puppy was burrowing next to my neck. Not understanding I struggled to become fully awake.

"What?" I mumbled.

Wally sat on the edge of the bed with a grin from ear to ear. "Meet Walter."

He helped me sit up and the puppy rolled down the pillow and into my lap, or what lap I had left. The puppy stood up and looked around in bewilderment. I laughed and scooped him up.

"Hello, Walter!" I said laughing. "As for you," I looked straight at Wally, "I'm gonna need more information."

Wally laughed, "Walter is your wedding present. I know most guys get their bride something like jewelry or a keepsake of some kind but I thought maybe, you could use a puppy."

I smelled his puppy fur and rubbed his head under my chin, "I love him!"

Walter cried all night until I put him up in the bed with me. Wally spooned me, I spooned Walter and we all fell asleep with a smile. Why was I worried about whether I was ready for marriage or not? Of course, I was ready! Wally, Bug, Walter, and I were going to have a beautiful life!

Chapter Thirty-Four

The big day was in two days! Mom and Dad arrived yesterday afternoon. Mom acted like she didn't really know how to react to me. She was making generic small talk and not very well. Dad was shadowing Wally. Wally went into the backyard; Dad went into the backyard. Wally got a drink from the fridge; Dad got a drink from the fridge. It was kind of cute but I could see it was making Wally uncomfortable. Mom wanted to know why we didn't find out the sex of the baby.

"After all, I'd like to know if I'm going to be a Grandma or a Grandpa," she said passionately.

"Well, Mom regardless, you're going to be a Grandma," I told her.

"But what if it's a boy?" she asked.

I decided further discussion was fruitless.

Wally's family arrived this afternoon. Gotta say, the parents weren't so keen on a mountain wedding but they respectfully kept their opinions to themselves. Wally's mother kept giving me 'the look'. I figured I'd just kill her with kindness.

Miss Vera was busy cooking and ordering the help around. Aunt Jo kept giving everyone 'the stink eye'. I told her to play nice. She pretty much kept to herself. I thought there would be somewhat of a reunion between her and my parents but they stayed away from each other, only speaking when necessary. My family tree was chock full of nuts. Lord, help the person who tried to shake the tree. Just ask Wally.

Corrie was channeling a wedding planner, I guess. All I know is that when she gave an order, everyone jumped to it with no questions asked. Somehow, through all the chaos, it was coming together.

The rehearsal and rehearsal dinner were tonight. Walter followed me every step. He was overjoyed with so many hands for petting. He trotted and strutted and stole everyone's heart. Wally had the idea that we could put a little bowtie on him and let him be the ring bearer. Wally's mom frowned but everyone else seemed to like the idea.

I was kind of wondering when the showdown with Wally's mom would come and I didn't have to wait long. At the dinner, there was excited conversation all around the table. Miss Vera outdid herself with baked salmon, a green salad, fresh sliced tomatoes swimming in mozzarella cheese, and balsamic vinegar. Large slices of toasted Texas Toast (homemade, of course) sopped up juices. For dessert, she had a beautifully decorated strawberry cream cake with buttercream frosting and tiny pink roses.

When we had stuffed ourselves and complimented a blushing Miss Vera, Wally's mom began picking up plates.

"I'll help!" I told her with a smile.

She turned and went into the kitchen. I followed her with an equally impressive stack of plates.

"How about you wash and I dry?" I suggested.

She turned to me and I nearly ran into her. "You should know, Probably, that I don't approve of this marriage. I don't know what you did to my boy but…" she began to cry.

Even though I was expecting a showdown, it still caught me off guard. "I didn't do anything to him," I said the first thing that came into my head.

"You get pregnant so he didn't have a choice?" her voice dripped with venom.

"No!" I exclaimed through my hurt. "Here, come sit down and let's talk."

She glared at me through the hatred but she finally sat down refusing to look at me.

"Mrs. Jenkins, Wally and I love each other…very much. I promise with all I have to promise with, there was no scheming or ulterior motives on my part."

"This wedding is a mockery of a very sacred tradition. Getting married in the woods? You pregnant for the whole world to see before the wedding? And a…a…*ghost hunter* to marry you? It flies in the face of the sanctity of marriage." Tears leaked from her eyes.

I used a second to organize my thoughts. She was right in some ways. Neither Wally nor I were taking any of this very seriously. We were treating it like it was nothing more than a big ol' party.

"I see why you think that," I said softly. "We're having it in the mountains because that's where we spend most of our time. We've had awesome adventures when we were in the mountains. Nature is very near and dear to our hearts. The pregnancy was an accident. No one was more shocked than me when I found out. Wally was over the moon. You know what he told me?"

She reluctantly shook her head still not looking at me.

"He said this baby is the best of both of us. That may not mean much to you but it meant the world to me. I've never been like other girls. I've never been sure exactly where I belonged. I've spent most of my growing-up years alone and I just figured I'd spend the rest of my life alone. Your son made me believe I was somebody. He made me believe in myself. He never gave up on me. I'm not going to be the usual daughter-in-law but I want you and Wally's father to become just as important to me as you are to your son. I promise you, through all the quirky episodes we're bound to have, and until the day I die, I will never intentionally hurt your son. Hurting him would be hurting myself. I would fight Satan himself to protect Wally." I thought about fighting Brendore and that was kind of like fighting Satan to protect Wally and our child.

"You really do love him?" she asked.

"I really do love him. Every cell, breath, and heartbeat, I love him," I answered. "I would like for you and I to be friends but I understand that I have a lifetime to prove to you that your son will never know what it's like to be alone or lonely. He will always know love," I said and danged if I didn't feel tears too. "Do you think that might be a possibility? Us becoming friends?"

In answer, she stood, came to me, and put her arms around me, "Welcome to the family. Now, let's talk about using that dog as a ring bearer."

She laughed but didn't pursue it. We cleaned Miss Vera's kitchen and could hear much laughing and celebrating in the living room.

"Sounds like they're having fun," she said. "Maybe we should join them."

"You go ahead. I'll be in in a minute," I hugged her again for good measure. "Thank you for talking to me. You can always talk to me. I'll do my best to tell you what you need to know."

She nodded then walked into the living room to join in the fun. I leaned against the kitchen counter. Tomorrow I was getting married. Snapshots of the past six years flashed in front of me. Sitting at this kitchen table countless times with those magical cinnamon rolls. Drinking oceans of hot tea together. That wild-haired skinny girl standing on the doorstep with a book in hand. Digging in the dirt to plant gardens. The ups and downs of a life well-lived. How would all this change? That's what kept me awake at night. I felt like a boulder was sitting in the pit of my stomach. How would my world change?

Walter came trotting in to see what I was up to. I scooped him up and he slurped my nose. I laughed. "You ready to be a ring bearer?" I asked him. He gently bit my nose. "Yeah, well, no eating the ring, okay? I don't think I could go through all this a second time."

I kissed him on the top of his head and set him down. Wally said he was a six-week-old Burmese Mountain Dog. He would get as big as Spirit, maybe bigger. Still, I looked forward to watching him grow and become a member of our family. He would be a wonderful big brother to the baby.

"You have awfully big shoes to fill, little buddy," I said wistfully. My heart still ached for Spirit but my life as I knew it was changing fast. I could either fear it or embrace it. Fear, the dragon that kept happiness at bay.

"You okay, babe?"

I looked up and saw Wally leaning against the doorframe.

I smiled at him, walked over, and kissed him, "More than you could ever know."

Chapter Thirty-Five

Have you ever laid in bed and it was so dark you could barely see your hand in front of your face? Then, in shades so subtle you couldn't differentiate when daylight seemed to creep in. Just suddenly, you realized you could see more and then more, and then there it was...the sunlight. That's the way I felt when I woke the next morning but it had nothing to do with daylight. I felt very subtle changes, changes I didn't see or maybe recognize at the time but changes I felt deep in my bones. Something had shifted. Some evolution was taking place, I just couldn't see it clearly yet but I could feel it and it scared the crap out of me.

I smelled bacon. I turned and touched the bed. It was room temperature so Wally had been up for a while. I lay on my back and contemplated the ceiling. Of course, things were different. Man, that bacon smelled good! Anyway, Brendore was no longer a threat...at least for the foreseeable future. Was that the shift? I wondered if Wally had fixed scrambled eggs or pancakes. Back to the pondering at hand. How much would my life change now? Would I no longer be visited by...Screw it! I'm going to go beg some breakfast! As I threw the covers back it hit me...I wasn't nauseous! I was hungry!

Overjoyed, I bounced out of bed, made a quick stop to pee, and went into the kitchen.

Wally turned around, "I'm sorry, babe. Are the smells getting to you?" He held tongs in his hand with a spatula in the other.

"It certainly did!" I laughed, "Load me up, and don't scrimp on the bacon."

We ate while talking and giggling as only a couple can do. When we finished every last crumb, I smiled at him, "Thank you."

"What are you thanking me for?" he asked.

"For being wonderful. For loving me. For being willing to take on my bizarre life. For this," I placed his hand on my tummy as Bug kicked and rolled across my belly. His smile said it all.

"Good morning, little Bug," he said to my baby bump. Bug's fist bulged my stomach, like she/he was giving Daddy a fist bump.

As we were cleaning up the kitchen, Miss Vera stuck her head in the back door.

"Ummm, Probably, can I talk with you?" she asked.

I gave her a little look because usually she just waltzed in without a thought. "Yeah, sure! Come on in!"

"Actually, I need you to come over to the house," she said mysteriously.

"Go on," Wally said giving Miss Vera a smooch on the cheek, "I'll finish up here."

"Okay, just let me get some decent clothes on and I'll be right there," I said.

Once again, I felt shifting sands beneath my soul. This was starting to creep me out.

As I headed for the door, Wally called out to me, "Don't forget, you have a wedding to get to in…four hours and…thirty-six minutes. Don't even think about not showing up."

Walter pranced beside me. Little stinker already knew who his treat supplier was. We walked over to Miss Vera's and I saw the little red scooter sitting in the driveway. Uh-oh, that can't be good.

I announced myself and Walter and I went into the house. I could hear talking in the kitchen so we headed straight for the source for treat dispensing.

"Hey, what's up?" I asked.

"We need to talk to you," Miss Vera said as she offered me a seat at the table. She had chocolate croissants and hot tea sitting on the table. She was using her very best china and had fresh flowers as a centerpiece. I kind of cocked my head. Now I was pretty sure I wasn't going to like this talk.

"You're getting married this afternoon," she began.

"Uh-huh," I said cautiously.

"You're starting a family!" she said with a wide smile.

"Is this an episode of This Is Your Life?" I asked.

"What Vera is trying NOT to say, is, it's over. Turn off the lights and pay the band," Aunt Jo said miserably.

"Jo! We agreed I would do the talking and you wouldn't," Miss Vera snapped.

Aunt Jo just slunk down in her chair.

"Over? What's over? And what band? There is no band!" I felt the panic start to squeeze my chest.

Miss Vera took a deep breath and glared at Aunt Jo, "Honey, you know how you've been helping all those poor spirits find Rest? Well, that was just a…a…side job, so to speak. Your destiny was…well…Brendore. That's why you had a protector. That's why I was your Coordinator and why Spirit came into your life. It was all to support your confrontation with Brendore."

"Yeah, so Brendore is gone. We can breathe easy for a while at least," I pointed out.

"Yes! You did wonderful!" Miss Vera crowed.

"So, what's the problem?" I really did not see where this was headed.

Miss Vera took a chocolate croissant and began to take it apart, layer by layer.

Aunt Jo sighed and took it away from her, "Our jobs are done and now it's time for us to go."

"Wait. What? Go where?" I could feel the tears stinging my eyes.

"We'll be given another assignment, I suppose," Miss Vera said softly. "Oh, Probably, I have grown to love you very much. This was never just an assignment for me. I truly love your heart, your funny ways, you and Wally together. I loved having you live in my garden shed, oh my gosh, I've loved every day!"

I was stunned. Never in a million years would I have seen this coming. I, naively, thought we would always be together. Miss Vera would be like a grandma to Bug, Aunt Jo would be the one to give Bug bad ideas and teach bad words, we would live in our little cottage and just be one big, happy family. To be honest, I wasn't all that sure I could live without them.

Aunt Jo interrupted my dismal thoughts, "Hey, look. Here's the thing, you grew on me, I'll give you that but you were a royal pain in the butt. No more tramping around in God's forgotten garden? No more having to fly halfway across the world to get your butt out of hot water? What's to miss?"

I looked at her and gave her a crooked smile, "I love you too, you old, dried-up bag of bones."

I felt my heart was made of cement and was much too heavy for my ribcage to hold. When I looked up to ask when all this was happening, you know, turning the lights out and paying the band, so to speak, I saw a tear slide down Aunt Jo's cheek. She swiped it away. Too late, I went to her and wrapped her in my arms…she hugged me back. Miss Vera was openly sobbing now. We shared a group hug.

"We're just tying up some loose ends and then…we'll have to say goodbye," Miss Vera said somberly. "It has been my greatest honor to spend these years, hours, minutes with you."

Okay, now I was having trouble holding back the tears.

"Ditto," Aunt Jo said without looking at me, "All that mushy crap."

Wally came to check to see what was taking so long and he saw three women hugging and crying all at once.

"Hey! There's no crying on my wedding day!" he exclaimed, "No crying! What happened? Aunt Jo, what have you done to Red now?"

Aunt Jo raised her head and glared at him then smiled. "Come here, you big lug," she said and included him in the hug.

When we had hugged and cried all we could, Wally asked again, "What happened?"

"We're turning off the lights and paying the band," I said.

"Huh?" he wrinkled his brow.

"I'll explain later," I could still feel my chin quivering.

Chapter Thirty-Six

I looked in the mirror and my thoughts drifted away like dandelion down. What a life these past six years had been. I didn't know if I would still be helping the lost souls find Rest or if that was the band I had paid. Today marked the beginning of a brand new chapter with different adventures, different challenges, different outcomes. There was a soft tap at my door.

"Who is it?" I answered.

"It's me, Red," Wally's sweet voice replied.

"You can't come in. Miss Vera said you can't see the bride," I said checking my hair.

There was a momentary silence and I thought he had gone away but then, "Umm...little late for that now, isn't it?"

I laughed, "Yeah, I guess it is. Come on in."

He opened the door and stopped. He stood stock-still. "Wow! You look beautiful!"

I felt my face flush with embarrassment, "Well, don't get used to it. This is the one and only time."

He was still staring.

"You came to tell me something?" I coaxed.

"Umm...yeah, yeah, wow. The trolleys have started taking the guests up to the clearing."

"Oh, okay," I glanced back to the mirror. "This is really happening, isn't it?"

Wally put his arms around me and kissed me on the forehead, "I am the luckiest man in the world. I can't wait to spend the rest of my life proving to you that you are my whole world...or worlds...whatever the case may be. I love you so much, Probably Magic Sarangoski."

"I love you too," I whispered.

"Your dad will come get you when everyone else has been taken up. I guess I'll see you in the woods then," he smiled at me and my heart melted again.

When he left, there was another tap on the door.

"Who is it?" I called with a giggle. I figured Wally forgot to tell me something.

The door opened and Catalina entered.

"Hey, Catalina!" I greeted her. "I'm so glad you came."

"Yeah, well, wouldn't miss it for the world and all that crap," she said, and then she really saw me. "You're really beautiful."

"Thank you," I blushed again.

"Red Probably Magic, I need your dragonfly necklace," she said.

"Why?" I asked as I fingered the delicate silver dragonfly. Wally had gotten this for me when we first started our friendship. For the last several years, it was never off of me.

"There's trouble brewing in the Realm. I want to give you protection," she said cryptically.

"Trouble? What kind of trouble?" I asked alarmed. Had Brendore escaped the gates of Hell?

"I'll not explain at this time but this will help protect you. Keep it on you at all times," she said as I handed her the necklace.

"Is it...you know what? That's not fair! I'm about to be married, have a child, losing Miss Vera and...wait a minute!

Miss Vera and Aunt Jo won't have to leave! Do they know? We have to tell them!" The joy I felt that maybe things wouldn't have to be so different. I would need a Protector and a Coordinator!

Catalina slowly shook her head. "I'm sorry, Red. I don't think they will be able to stay. They had an assignment and that assignment is over." She handed the necklace back. "By the way, congratulations on your marriage."

She looked so sad. I wondered if her father's curse had finally been lifted from her, would she finally find a love of her own.

She touched my arm, "My father was evil, Red. You didn't 'take my father' away from me. Brendorc was full of hatred and anger. As far as I'm concerned, he didn't get anywhere near the punishment he deserved. Don't feel sorry for me. I'm free and that's something I've wanted my entire existence but it does come with a price. I'm willing to pay it. As for you, I think of you as a friend and I want to offer you protection for whatever may happen in the Realm as it affects you."

"Catalina…" I started but she had vanished. I stood stunned and worried. What else could happen today? I shouldn't have thrown that challenge out in the universe as there was another tap on the door.

"What?" I shouted in frustration.

Dad stuck his head around the door, "You ready? The trolley is here."

"Yeah, as ready as I'll ever be," I said as I picked up my bouquet of white roses and green ivy.

"You look radiant," he smiled.

"Thanks, you too," I said.

We took our seats on the trolley. Dad leaned over and kissed me on the cheek. That was a first! We were not an overly affectionate family. We didn't go for a lot of public display of affection. The simple sweet gesture brought tears.

"I love you, Daddy," I said over the lump in my throat.

"I love you too, Probably. I'm so proud of you," he said as he patted my hand. "Wally seems like a good and decent man. I think he'll be good to you."

"I think so too," I murmured.

We arrived at the clearing and I lifted my skirt so I didn't trip on my dress. If anyone thought they would get a glimpse of a glamorous shoe fit for a bride, they would be sorely disappointed. I was wearing my hiking boots scuffs, chew marks on the soles, and all.

I put pressure on my father's arm before we began our processional to the front. I just wanted to take a moment and drink it all in. The smell of crisp leaves and the promise of fall scented the air. There was an arch covered in white roses with tiny pink rosebuds wound throughout. Light green and pale rose ribbons fell from bows tucked among the flowers. Rosa wore a pale rose floor-length gown, as my maid of honor. Corrie and Adrian, Wally's sister, wore pale green knee-length gowns. They had flowers woven into their hair. Wally was looking off into the forest. Our friend, Cube, the Kentucky State Trooper, had hold of Walter who wore a bow tie with a small jewelry box tied to it. Cube smiled and barely nodded. I smiled back at him.

There weren't a lot of guests but enough. And then as I watched the guests, new guests arrived. I saw Jacob and Vesta, Claire Roman, Peter Euclid, and Rosa Hargate, Otis Smoot with a beaming Primrose, Bob McCoy, the patrons of the magic show, they were all there. They looked so happy. Mom sat in the front row on the bride's side and Wally's parents sat in the front row on the groom's side. Music was playing from speakers placed discreetly in trees. I took a very deep breath and took my first step toward a new life. Uncle Dave stood with hands folded, ready to officiate the vows. Walter trotted up the aisle, stopping to sniff first one person then another. Miss Vera secretly slipped him a little treat. He eventually made it to Wally and sat panting and grinning as Wally's brother untied the ribbon from his collar.

"We are gathered here to witness the marriage of Wallace Canton Jenkins and Probably Magic Sarangoski. Who gives this woman to be married?" Uncle Dave began.

"Her mother and I do," Dad said hoarsely. He placed my hand in Wally's, kissed me on the cheek again, and joined my mother.

Wally had two long-stemmed red roses which he presented to our mothers.

The ceremony was short and sweet. No Brendore, no Manoucks, nothing but happy faces and a few tears.

After the ceremony, we went back to Miss Vera's house. White canopies were set up in the field behind the house. Tables of food and tables for the guests were decorated with tall white candles with rosebud garlands wound around them. A band had set up in front with a constructed dance floor for those who wanted to dance the night away.

The cake. Oh my gosh, the cake! It was four tiers high with white icing and fresh flowers cascading down it like a waterfall. The flowers were Hydrangeas, Freesia, and small yellow roses. It was almost too beautiful to eat.

I was dancing with Wally when I happened to catch a glimpse of Miss Vera and Aunt Jo. They were walking away from the festivities. I could barely hear them talking.

"That was a beautiful ceremony," Miss Vera said.

"Lot of hoopla for nothing," Aunt Jo grumbled.

Miss Vera turned and looked at her, "We are definitely going to have to work on your people skills."

Aunt Jo looked insulted, "MY people skills? There's absolutely nothing wrong with my people skills. I got great skills!"

"Maybe for an ill-tempered badger," Miss Vera giggled.

I saw Aunt Jo take her foot and playfully tap Miss Vera's bottom.

Their voices faded and so did they. They were just gone. My heart felt like it was going to break but then perhaps we'd meet again someday. One just never knew what kind of adventure life would take us on.

I lay my head on Wally's shoulder as we swayed to the slow music and the stars began to appear. One just never knew.

Other Books in the Probably Magic Series

Probably Magic: A Letter for Rosa

Probably Magic: The Wheel of Misfortune

Probably Magic: The Seventh Magic Marble

Probably Magic: Two-Faced

If you enjoyed this story, please be so kind as to leave a review on Amazon.com and any of your favorite book nooks. Reviews are the lifeblood for authors.

I invite you to also check out the first series, The Old Man and The Watch.

Book One: The Old Man and The Watch: Searching For the Long Road HOME

Book Two: The Good Guardian: The Battle of Grey Island

Book Three: SnakeSkin: Alone in the Time Zone

Book Four: The Glory Plains: The Raising of a Thousand Voices

Book Five: Tale of Oak: Coming HOME

Author Jo Jewell

I call myself a mountain woman. In truth, I was born on the flatlands of Indiana on May 20th, 1955. The world population was 2.780 billion, Eisenhower was President, unemployment was 5.5%, Cher was nine years old on that day, and you could mail a letter for .03 cents. Luckily, the dinosaurs were gone, and fire had been invented by then. I moved to Tennessee to the foot of The Great Smoky Mountains in 1998.

I have been writing since the age of six. I won my first regional poetry contest in second grade. For the past 50+ years, I have written for myself and only a chosen few. Writing to me is as life-sustaining as breathing, as important as a beating heart. I have written for newspapers, had my own local column in the Blount County Voice, shared stories of my life for my friends to make them laugh, sigh, cry, or more importantly, to think. I wrote puppet shows for our mentally handicapped facility, inspirational short stories for church services, and a series of articles that led to testimony before the Maryland State Senate and the creation of the bill: Maryland Task Force for Abused, Abandoned, and Neglected Children. As long as it meant I could write, I wrote. I can't tell you where this passion came from, I can't tell you one incident that caused me to start writing and not stop. I have no memory of "starting" to write, I just did, and at a very early age.

I hope you enjoy reading this story as much as the characters enjoyed telling their stories.

CPSIA information can be obtained
at www.ICGtesting.com
Printed in the USA
BVHW032236080921
616210BV00019B/66